A KIMMEY KRUSE MYSTERY

FUNNY

AS A

DEAD COMIC

Susan Rogers Cooper

A THOMAS DUNNE BOOK

St. Martin's Press
New York

Design by Lynn Newmark

Library of Congress Cataloging-in-Publication Data

Cooper, Susan Rogers.
    Funny as a dead comic / Susan Rogers Cooper
      p.   cm.
    "A Thomas Dunne book."
    ISBN 0-312-09815-4
    1. Women detectives—Illinois—Chicago—Fiction.
    2. Women comedians—Illinois—Chicago—Fiction.
    3. Chicago (Ill.)—Fiction.   I. Title.
    PS3553.06235F8   1993
    813'.54—dc20   93-24384
                                            CIP

First Edition: November 1993

10 9 8 7 6 5 4 3 2 1

To
Elaine Riggs Edgington
and
Kathy Gattis Alexander
whose combined strength of
character and scathing
sense of humor have kept me in line
for longer than any of us
would care to remember

ACKNOWLEDGMENTS

I would like to express my sincere appreciation to my good friend, stand-up comedian Debbie Tate, for her invaluable assistance on the nuts and bolts of a comic's life. Also, a warm thank-you to my friend Marilyn Newcom, a bottomless pit of truly tasteless jokes

I would also like to thank those gracious people, other writers, who have read, reread, and re-reread this manuscript and have all come to the conclusion that I am the worst speller to ever put pen to paper. Cindy Bonner, Mary Willis Walker, Jan Grape, Barbara Burnett Smith, Susan Wade, and Dinah Chenven. Again, sisters, those were not misspellings—only typos.

Thanks as always to my wonderful editor, Ruth Cavin, and a special thank you to my agent, Richard Curtis, for taking the chance. As always, my love and appreciation to my husband, Don, and my daughter, Evin, for giving me the time and space needed to be another person for a little while.

FUNNY
AS A
DEAD
COMIC

1

I looked at my reflection in the mirror, my first day of my daily affirmations. "You're funny," I told the lady looking back "You're very, very funny. You are a funny woman." The reflection said, "Funny looking, maybe." The image looking back, complete with oversized UT football jersey and Bullwinkle bedroom slippers, bore out the complaint.

I threw myself dramatically across the hotel-room bed. No one was there to see the high drama as I reached across and picked up the phone, dialing the ten digits I knew by heart.

Phoebe picked up on the fourth ring. "What?"

"Why did I dye my hair red?" I wailed.

"Because you have a Lucille Ball complex."

"That's probably true. Did I tell you Cab Neusberg's headlining tomorrow night?"

"About a thousand times. Did I mention that it's four o'clock in the morning here?"

I rolled over on my back. "Yeah, here, too. What am I gonna do about Cab?"

"Drool?" Phoebe's always been the queen of snappy patter.

"This is a very delicate situation," I whined. "How can I go up in front of millions of people . . ."

"Since when have you ever had an audience of more than fifty?"

"Great, Phoeb. Simply destroy all my confidence!"

"What confidence?"

"This phone call is not helping," I said.

"It's four o'clock in the morning."

"I know. I couldn't sleep."

"Well I could and I was. Good night, Kimmey. Break a leg and whatever else is appropriate."

The line went dead in my hand.

I met Phoebe Love the first day of school at Lamar Junior High, Austin, Texas, in the fall of 1976. I was totally lost and about to burst into tears. So was Phoebe, but I didn't know that until years later. She took me by the shoulder strap of my Whole Earth Provisions knapsack (my parents were liberals), and walked me around the perimeter of the school twice, blithely telling me the specialties of each room. She was totally wrong, of course, but I thought she was the coolest person who ever lived. Unfortunately, I still do.

She was born Phoebe Saperstein-Lowell two years before Woodstock, to which her parents dragged her. After that, they legally changed her name to Phoebe Rainbow Love. She has since dropped the *a-i-n-b-o-w* from her middle name and now simply goes by Phoebe R. Love. Sort of like Toys "R" Us.

I turned off the light and crawled under the covers and pretended to sleep. Tomorrow was going to be a bitch. At the time, I didn't know just how big a bitch.

The Kaiser Komedy Klub was new. Well, a new club in an old building, in the general vicinity of most of the other clubs in Chicago, in Old Town. Chicago's finest, they called themselves. That remained to be seen. It was my first gig at the Kaiser. Of course, it was everybody else's first one, too. I knew Bert Kaiser, the owner, from when he worked at Second City. Not that I've ever performed at Second City. I mean, I've been there, but only as audience. But Bert Kaiser was someone everybody knew. He wasn't with SC long—less than a year—but he's been in the biz, on the edges, around, since Henny Youngman was funny. So when Myra Mitchell, my agent, called me in Austin to say she got me a gig at Bert Kaiser's new club, I said, sure. I figured with Bert, I might get paid. There are some clubs where you go out there on a leap of faith, not knowing if the term *professional comedian* will apply this time or not.

That night, at the Kaiser Komedy Klub, the lineup was a bit unusual. Five comedians instead of the usual three. Generally, the pecking order is first the "opener," who is usually the lowest paid, has the hardest job, and is expected to lick the boots of both the middle and the headliner. The headliner gets to have his or her boots licked by both the middle and the opener, unless there is a personality conflict or drug use involved, in which case the majority rules, sometimes resulting in mean and vengeful actions toward the outsider. It's a fun life.

But for his grand opening, Bert Kaiser had gone for broke: two openers, me and Bobby Rivers, whom I'd worked with at the Laugh Stop in Houston (California chic/generic funny); two middles, Babe Marsh, a lady I'd worked with once on the Jersey Shore, three hundred pounds' worth of fat jokes, and Joey Scarlotti, a New York City Italian I'd only seen on Letterman (Andrew Dice Clay without the warmth) but never worked with; and the headliner, of course, was none other than Cab Neusberg.

I hadn't seen Cab in three years. Not since the Laff-a-Lot in Denver. Okay, so Cab and I had been lovers. Well, not exactly lovers. We'd slept together. Okay, so we didn't exactly sleep, but we did have an exceedingly nice one-night stand the last night of the L-a-L. You may wonder why I'd take a gig knowing Cab Neusberg was going to be there after three years of silence. Am I a glutton for punishment? Did I want to have a scene? Did I wonder if he'd remember my name? The last one was a possibility.

I am not promiscuous. As a matter of fact, at the ripe old age of twenty-eight, I've only slept with five men. A late bloomer, my first was in my freshman year at the University of Texas. His name was Keith and the entire experience was so boring it took me until my senior year to repeat it. But then it was Billy.

Sex with Billy was anything but boring. We moved in together after two months and were together almost three years. Billy convinced me that sex could be fun. I convinced him he was gay. He left me for a guy named Warren.

By that time I was out of school and working as an investigator for a medical malpractice insurance company. David was my supervisor. He let me cry on his shoulder about Billy and then married me. Sex with David was as interesting as it had been with Keith. But the good thing about David was that I made him laugh. I'd work on routines in my head at the office and later that night in bed, for want of anything better to do, I'd try them out on him. When I decided to try my living at making others laugh, David and I split up. We're still friends, though. He's getting married next month to Shirley, another investigator at the old insurance office, and I'm invited. And I'll go, too, if I don't have a gig.

Number four was someone I met on the road my first year as a comic. Okay, so I don't remember his name, if I ever knew. I'm slightly ashamed of that. I am not ashamed of the fact that I found out my body had the capacity for multiple orgasms. That was in Cleveland. I think. I did some drinking that first year on the road. Most of it's a blur.

My fifth and last lover was Cab Neusberg at the Denver L-a-L. The L-a-L lasted four days. We flirted for three. Cab's a rarity in nineties comedy—a political satirist. He's basically not a funny man. Very intense. His gripes are real—exaggerated, of course, but real. Physically he's also a rarity in comedy. Stand-up comedy is one of the few places in show business where one doesn't have to be pretty to succeed. Being "funny looking" is a plus. Not for Cab. He was six foot four inches tall, slender, with one of those worked-up bodies with pecs and fine ripples in his back. He had curly, dark brown hair, worn long, past his collar, moss green eyes that pulled you in and kept you there, and dimples. He had a wonderful, wide, generous mouth, an aristocratic nose, and his legs were gorgeous. Okay, so maybe I took the gig because Cab Neusberg wasn't completely out of my system. Even after three years of silence.

I was sitting in the green room with Joey Scarlotti and Babe Marsh, while Bobby Rivers opened the evening, when Cab came in. In the three years since our time together at the Denver Laff-a-Lot, nothing much had changed. He was still beautiful. The only difference was that now he was hot and getting rich and had "people."

There was a woman in a power suit, about forty, with straight, blunt-cut frosted hair, a cigarette in one hand, and a time organizer in the other. Central casting agent/manager. And there was a guy, Cab's age—mid-thirties—with short, fuzzy hair and middle European ancestry two generations back, who laughed at everything Cab said. Or thought, possibly. Obviously his assistant. Which meant he got the girls, got rid of the girls, paid the girls, checked the girls' ages, etc. A very important part of any up-and-comer's entourage.

Okay, so my stomach did a one-eighty into my liver at the sight of him. It happens. He was the most beautiful son-of-a-gun I'd ever slept with. Also the sexiest. Also, and this I wouldn't admit to just anybody, he was nice. Intense, but nice. Not nice enough to call in three years but . . .

I turned quickly when he came in. My back was to him and I pretended to be studying a three-week-old issue of *Time*. I could hear him behind me making cracks with the club emcee, Mickey Reynolds, and to Joey and Babe.

"And this," Mickey said, laying a hand lightly on my shoulder, "is . . ."

I looked up into moss green eyes. "You don't have to introduce Kimmey to me," Cab said, smiling, dimples blazing in that beautiful face. "We're old friends."

He held out his hand and I took it, watching him mock bow over it, touching it lightly to his lips. I was once again glad I'd been born a woman, as it would have been embarrassing going out on stage in the male equivalent of my physical condition.

"Hey, Cab," I said, huskying up my voice in a bad imitation of Kathleen Turner, "how you doing?"

He sat down next to me, waving his hand in such a way as to dismiss the others. I loved it.

"Good." He grinned. "How are you?"

I shrugged. "Can't complain."

He touched my hair, which was red now, permed, and past my shoulders. "You changed your hair."

"Like it?" I asked.

He laughed. "It's bigger than you are."

His reference was to the fact that I'm more than a foot shorter than he is and have been fighting most of my life to put weight *on,* which ticks off every woman I know.

"Yeah, well, in this business—"

In unison, we said, "Ya gotta get noticed."

He traced a finger down my cheek. "What are you doing after?"

"Curling up in my hotel room with a bad book."

"Need some help turning the pages?"

I was saved from a snappy comeback by Mickey calling me. "Kimmey, you're on deck."

"See ya, Cab," I said, getting up to leave.

"Sooner than you'd imagine."

I sloshed out to the wings to watch Joey finish insulting everyone who'd ever lived.

It didn't go well that night. Some nights are diamonds, some nights are toe-jam. Sometimes the audiences aren't in the collective mood, sometimes the material doesn't work, sometimes I'm a little off. That night, I was a lot off. Instead of thinking of airline jokes, men-bashing, and parent-poking, I was thinking about Cab Neusberg. And whether or not he should go back with me to the hotel to, excuse the expression, turn my pages.

Was I satisfied to be the poke in this port? The sure thing? Was I so horny I was willing to put my pride on hold for a sleazy one-night stand with Cab Neusberg? You can bet your butt I was.

The nearness of yours truly didn't seem to bother Cab's performance that night at the Kaiser Komedy Klub. He was brilliant. As usual. Took the house down. Had 'em stomping and shouting, laughing and clapping. Even in the wings. I couldn't take my eyes off him. But still he made me laugh. He always does. When Cab's performing, I don't think about his timing, how he could have changed this word or that word to make the bit funnier. I just go with it. Let it flow over me. And laugh my butt off.

I was back in the green room when the gofer/assistant/girl-checker/whatever came to get me.

"Hey, beautiful," he said, smiling and taking my hand in his. "He's waiting."

I could tell by his grip on my hand that I was supposed to stand. I rarely do things I'm supposed to do. My mother can attest to that. "I beg your pardon?" I said, putting as much Texas in my voice as I could muster.

He let go of my hand. His smile was still there, but it was weakening. "Cab's waiting in the bus."

I knew Cab was traveling now in one of those customized buses that country and western singers seem to like. Great, I thought, a quickie in the Pullman of his frigging bus.

I stood up and walked toward the door. "Tell Cab I'm staying at the Lake House."

"Ah . . . wait . . . Kimmey . . . Ms. Kruse . . ."

I turned. He smiled and stuck out his hand. "I didn't introduce myself," the sleaze said. "I'm Bucky Schwartz. I'm Cab's assistant. He asked that I escort you to the bus, so if you're ready. . . ."

I laughed. "Tell Cab I'm at the Lake House. Room four-eleven. He can find me there. Nice meeting you . . . Bucky."

I took a taxi to the Lake House, a nice name for a nasty little hotel so far from the lake you couldn't even smell the pollution. But it was okay because I knew the owners, Tracy and Max Jones, expatriot Texans, trying to make it in Chi-town. Tracy,

Phoebe, and I had roomed together in college; therefore, I always had a place to stay in Chicago.

I always got the same room at the Lake House, fourth floor, five rooms from the elevator, a king-size bed, a desk, and a love seat, with a view of the back of another building. Which beat the hell out of the front rooms' view—a busy, noisy, congested four-lane street topped off by the overpass of one of Chicago's many, many freeways.

The only good thing about the Lake House—other than the fact that I got to stay there free—was its history. It had originally been built at the turn of the century. Somewhere around the late teens, most of it had burned to the ground. The remodeling was done in the early twenties when it was bought by a gangster as a safe house/cathouse. There had been girls in every room and trapdoors in every other room, making for quick escapes in case the feds or rival gangs showed up. Max and Tracy had found a few pictures of the hotel in those days of the rip-roaring twenties and had them prominently displayed in the lobby.

Once ensconced in my room, I took a shower and changed into a black teddy I always packed, for moral support, I guess. This was the first time in three years I'd put it on. I looked around the room, wondering if it would beat Cab's bus as a love nest. There was a semibald chenille bedspread (multi-colored, if you considered white with various shades of stain "colored") over a fifties modern Hollywood bed; a love seat covered in a burnt or-ange and hot pink peacock-feather print; and a painting over the bed of big-eyed children (one boy and one girl—one black, one white), the little girl holding a big-eyed cat. Okay, so it wasn't exactly the honeymoon suite at the No-Tell Motel on Highway Six in Cut and Shoot, Texas, but it would have to do.

The knock came on the door at one-fifteen. I checked the peephole, half expecting Bucky's eye to peek back at me. No, this eye was moss green. I opened the door.

"Hey," he said, leaning against the doorjamb, smiling just enough for one dimple to shine through. "Sorry if Bucky gave you the wrong idea."

"Well, hell, Cab, he didn't drag me by the hair to the sultan's tent, so what the hey . . ."

He leaned forward and kissed me lightly on the lips. "Looking good, Kimmey."

I opened the door to let him in. I'm not made of stone, folks. He looked around the room, then looked back at me. "Why don't you give this up and start touring with me in my bus? We'll make it a team thing. . . ."

"Sure, Cab, after my performance tonight, I can really see you wanting to do that."

He shook his head. "I've been keeping track of your career, babe. You were off tonight. So what? You're usually right on. Usually got them eating out of your pretty little hand."

He picked up said pretty little hand and nibbled on it. "I've missed you."

So what kind of third-grade, numb-nuts virgin would fall for a line like that? After three years of total silence? Okay, my kind.

Our clothes were off in record time, the covers rumpled. He was on top of me, we were making love, when, all of a sudden, he shuddered and stopped. Five minutes, tops. Not the old Cab Neusberg I knew. He lay silently on top of me, his head resting on my right shoulder, all his weight, all one hundred and seventy-some pounds, mashing me against the bedding.

"Cab?" I said, pushing at him gently. "Honey, you wanna roll over now?" I pushed a little harder. "Cab? Come on, babe, you're squishin' me."

I turned toward his head, seeing only the back of it. With my free hand, the one not pinned under him, I turned his face toward me. His eyes were closed, his mouth open, saliva seeping out from between his teeth.

I wiggled under him. "Cab? Damn, Cab, get off!" I don't know why I did it. I wasn't really thinking straight. But, with my free hand, I pressed my fingers against his carotid artery. Nothing moved, nothing stirred in there. No pulse. Nothing.

I gagged and shoved, moving him only slightly. I wiggled and squirmed, using my legs and free arm to pry him up. Finally, after what seemed forever, I got out from under him and sat there on the bed staring at him. I lifted his hand and felt for his pulse. It still wasn't there. Cab Neusberg was dead.

'm an only child. No siblings. But I do have two
parents. And four grandparents. One great
grandma. Five aunts, four uncles, twelve first
cousins, sixteen great-aunts, seven great-uncles,
and a plethora of second, third and removed cousins. What I'm trying to say is, we don't die much in
my family. And, because of this, the first dead body
I'd ever seen in my life happened to be lying in my
bed.

I don't know how long I sat there staring at Cab
before I slipped my teddy back on and picked up
the phone to call the front desk. My friend Max, the
owner, answered.

"Max, this is Kimmey—"

"Do you know what Texas foreplay is?" Max
asked.

"Not now, Max, listen—"

"It's when the man says, 'Honey, you awake? Oh, well, it don't matter anyway.' "

Max laughed uproariously. One thing about being a professional comedian is that people insist on telling you jokes. Quite often at the most inopportune times.

"Max, there's a dead man in my bed," I said.

"Yeah?" I could hear the grin in his voice, waiting for the punchline.

"Please call the police or something. Maybe an ambulance. But that won't help much," I said.

"Kimmey?"

"Yes, Max?"

"Is this supposed to be funny?"

"Funny as a dead comic." I hung up and pulled my blue jeans up over my black teddy and pulled on a baggy sweater. Then I went and sat on the love seat and looked out the window at the building across the alley. It beat the hell out of looking at the dead body on the bed.

I heard the doorknob rattle and then the tentative knock on the door. "Kimmey?" Tracy, Max's wife, said. "Kimmey?"

I got up and moved slowly toward the door as Tracy's master key turned the lock. She walked in and looked at me. Then at the bed.

"Oh, my goodness," she said, seeing Cab.

"He didn't even die with a smile on his face," I said, then promptly burst into tears.

"I can't believe it," Phoebe said.

"I know," I wailed. "I know."

"Honey, I'm so sorry."

"I know, I know."

"You want me to fly up there?"

I gulped in air and sobbed one last sob. "No. No, really. Tracy and Max are here."

"Do the authorities know what happened?" Phoebe asked.

I shook my head, then said, "No. Not yet. They just got him out of here. You shoulda seen the jerk EMTs. Practically smirking."

"Well, if you were in their shoes . . ."

"I would have been sensitive."

"You woulda said something like, Whata way to go." She was silent. "Wouldn't you, Kimmey?"

I sighed. "Yes, I would have. But that doesn't mean I wouldn't have been a jerk, too."

"That's true."

"Why is it talking to you on the phone is not what I ever envision it to be?"

"Reality is a cruel master," Phoebe said.

"What do I do now?"

"Get another room and get some sleep."

"Yeah. I guess you're right."

"Kimmey?"

"Yeah?" I asked, tentatively, knowing what was coming.

"What a way to go, huh?"

"Bitch."

"I love you, you wanton woman."

"I love you, too, slut."

I hung up and grabbed my bag out of the closet and began packing it up, then called the desk to see if there was a room they could move me to. I wasn't particularly worried. Except for me, the two hookers on the first floor with rooms rented by the hour, and the novelty-items salesman on three, the hotel was empty.

Tracy came up and helped me move my stuff. "The cops said they'd get back to us in the morning. They might know something about how . . . well, you know," Tracy said.

I'd known Tracy since our freshman year at UT. She and Phoebe and I shared a room at Dobie Towers. Tracy was from Lufkin. Actually, she was a cheerleader at Lufkin High and Tracy didn't believe in talking about anything negative. Therefore, when any subject came up involving nasty things like death, crime, taxes, bad hair, etc., she avoided the topic whenever possible.

"About how and why Cab died?" I asked. Phoebe was right. Reality-check time.

"Well, yes, I guess."

She hauled my bag down three rooms and opened the door with the key she then handed me.

"So," Tracy said, all smiles, "tomorrow's another day."

I went into the new room, got out of the jeans and sweater, and was standing there in the teddy. Then I took that off and put on the old UT football jersey I usually wear to bed. I thought about burning the teddy. A sort of symbolic gesture. Maybe scatter the ashes . . . never mind.

I lay in bed and thought about Max and Tracy. It was better than thinking about Cab Neusberg.

Max had come to UT for graduate school straight from East Texas State University. ETSU isn't a "black school"; actually, it's a state school. But the majority of the students are African-American. A lot of northeast Texas is black, with many small towns coming very close to putting up signs saying NO WHITES ALLOWED IN TOWN AFTER DARK at the city limits.

Max came to UT an angry, militant African-American. He was going to show UT a thing or two. He joined every organization with an exclusively black roster and set about protesting anything protestable. Phoebe and I met him at a "Free South Africa" rally on campus. We went across to the drag to a coffee shop afterwards and argued till they closed. Max was a great arguer. Then Phoebe and I made the fatal mistake of introducing him to Tracy.

The closest Tracy had ever gotten to a black man was her mother's maid's four-year-old son. Max took one look at blond, blue-eyed Tracy and began sagging. He started missing meetings and started walking her to class. Tracy could say the most outrageous white-bread things and Max would just smile and nod his head. They were married a month later. Tracy's parents hit the ceiling. Max's mother passed out and it took days to revive her. His militant friends disowned him; her sorority sisters blackballed her. I don't think Max and Tracy ever noticed. They inherited the hotel from a renegade uncle of Tracy's who'd won it in a poker game and they've been trying valiantly to run it for the past five years.

Somehow they managed. But mostly they just loved each other. I've always wanted a relationship like Max and Tracy's. To love somebody so much that all else dimmed beside it. I couldn't help wondering if my last chance at that kind of love had just dropped dead in my bed.

* * *

The phone woke me. I reached for it on the left, thinking I was in my old room, but in this room the phone was on the right. It rang four times before I managed to pick it up.

"Yes? Hello?"

"Kimmey?" The raspy voice I heard could only belong to one person: Bert Kaiser.

"Bert?"

"Jesus H. Christ. I just heard. Je . . . *sus* H. Christ on a bicycle. What happened?"

"He's dead, Bert."

"That I know. You okay, kid?"

"Yeah, I guess. How'd you find out?" I asked.

"The cops just called. They want everybody working last night here at three o'clock. That includes you, kid. You up to it?"

"Three o'clock?" I looked at the clock by the phone. It was a little after noon. "Yeah, I'll be there."

"Good girl. How about tonight? You gonna be able to go on?"

One didn't blow a gig just because a lover happened to drop dead on top of one. It wasn't done. "Yeah, no problem. The show must go on and all that."

"That'sa girl. I always said you got a truckload of moxy, kid. I always said that."

"I'll see you at three o'clock, Bert."

"In the green room. Bye, kid, and sorry, ya know?"

"Yeah, bye, Bert."

I got up and went into the bathroom, tinkled, and washed my face with cold water. Then I looked at it. My face, I mean. My eyes were carrying bags the size of footlockers and they were rimmed in red from all the crying. There was a new line around my mouth. I looked more like forty-eight than twenty-eight. After a quick shower and hair wash, I got out my makeup bag and went to work. An hour later, I went downstairs to the coffee shop.

Max and Tracy had more business in the coffee shop than they ever had in the hotel. I mean where else in Chicago could you get real chicken fried steak, real barbecue, and honest to God Moon Pie?

Max was working behind the counter so I took one of the stools and plopped down. He leaned over and kissed my cheek.

"How ya doing, babe?" he asked.

I shrugged. "Do I look human?"

"You're always gorgeous to me, babe."

"And you've always been a great liar."

He poured me a cup of coffee and leaned across the counter. "I got something to take your mind off your troubles."

"What's that?"

"This bear goes into this bar to buy a beer, see—"

"Max!" Tracy came up behind him and nudged him in the ribs. "Not now!"

"What? She needs a distraction. Right, Kimster?"

I smiled weakly. "Yeah, I guess." I looked at Tracy. "It's okay . . ."

"Anyway," Max said, "this bear goes into this bar to buy a beer. The bartender says, 'I'm sorry, we don't serve beer to bears in bars. . . .' "

Tracy groaned as she hefted a plate of the luncheon special from the kitchen window. "Jeez, honey, not that one!"

"Shh . . ." Max waved her away. "Anyway, the bear roars and says, 'Look at me! I'm big, I'm bad and I want a beer!' But the bartender says, 'I'm sorry, we don't sell beers to bears in bars.' So the bear looks around, see, and he spots a lady at the end of the bar. He grabs her up, tears her head off, and eats her. Then he pounds the bar with his fist and says, 'Now will you give me a beer?' And the bartender goes, 'No, we don't serve beers to bears in bars. Especially bears that are on drugs.' The bear says, 'What do you mean on drugs?' And the bartender says, 'What about that bar-bitch-you-ate?' "

I groaned and Max laughed until I thought he'd choke. Finally, he said, "That's a good one, huh?"

I said, "Yes, Max, that's a good one. Very amusing."

Max frowned at me. "You take all the fun out of telling jokes."

"Food, Max."

He reached behind him and brought out my usual: a double-meat cheeseburger with chili and onions, a side of fries, a side of onion rings, and a strawberry malt.

"I don't think I can eat much today," I said. "Under the circumstances." I handed him back the onion rings.

I took a taxi to the Kaiser Komedy Klub, Binacaing all the way. I love onions. I really do. And garlic. Have you ever had an onion and garlic sandwich on white bread with hot mustard? It is to die for, I swear!

I was the last one to arrive. Three of the four

comedians I'd worked with the night before were over in a corner, Bobby and Joey sharing the couch, Babe taking up a love seat all by herself. Cab's gofer, Bucky Schwartz, was standing by one of the makeup tables, looking glum, and the lady I'd seen with Cab earlier, the agent/manager type, was talking on a cellular phone, her expensively clad hip resting on a table by the back wall. Mickey Reynolds, the club emcee, saw me as I came in and ran up and hugged me.

"Sweetie, you okay?" he asked, holding me at arm's length to look deep into my eyes.

I nodded. I noticed Joey Scarlotti punch Bobby Rivers and both laughed. Babe Marsh shushed them, then they all turned to look at me. This was gonna be more fun than picking okra, I could tell.

I found a chair away from everybody and sat down, staring at the floor. A shadow fell at my feet. I looked up into Bucky Schwartz's red-rimmed eyes.

"What happened last night?" he demanded, his voice unusually loud in the now totally quiet room.

All eyes turned toward the two of us. I sank back in the chair.

"He was perfectly all right when I dropped him off at your hotel! What the hell happened?" Bucky grabbed my arm.

A hand went over his and pulled my arm free. I looked up at a new face.

"And you are?" the new face asked Bucky.

Bucky jerked his hand away. "Who wants to know?"

The new face pulled a leather folder from the

inside pocket of his polyester suit and flipped a badge at the gofer.

"Detective Sal Pucci, Chicago PD."

Bucky said, "Oh," then held out his hand. "I'm Bucky Schwartz. I was Cab Neusberg's executive assistant." He turned toward me. "And this is Kimmey Kruse. The last person to see Cab alive."

I jumped up. "Now just a damn minute . . ."

Detective Pucci turned toward me. "You're the woman who was with Mr. Neusberg when he expired?"

"Yes, Detective Puzzi—"

"Pucci. Like Gucci. The shoe people?"

"Right. Anyway, yes, I was with Cab. But—"

"Have a seat, Ms. Kruse. I'll talk to you in a little bit." He turned and addressed the room in general. "Everybody, please just have a seat. For those of you who didn't hear, I'm Detective Pucci and I've been assigned to this case. I'm going to need to speak to each of you individually. It will take some time but we'll try not to keep anybody here too long. I'd appreciate some confidentiality from those I speak with. Okay?" All the heads in the room nodded in agreement. He rubbed his hands together. "Now, those are the ground rules. I guess we'll start with Ms. Kruse."

Joey and Bobby snickered again, until Detective Pucci shot them a look. He was an Al Pacino type. Short, swarthy. He had a receding hairline, a thin nose, and dark, brooding eyes. I've always preferred a man at least twice my size. Like the old Julie Brown song says, "I like 'em big and stupid." Not that I was shopping. But we single women notice these things. It's genetic. Pucci was around five feet six or seven inches tall, somewhere between thirty-five and forty, and had no ring on the ring finger of his left hand. I've been single for most of my twenty-eight years. It's second nature to notice these things.

I stood up and followed Detective Pucci out of the room.

"Your boss has been kind enough to lend us his office," he said, once we were in the hall.

"My boss?"

"Bert Kaiser. Isn't he your boss?"

I snorted. "Hardly. He's a club owner. I'm a co-median. He hires me to work the club for two or three nights. Okay, technically, maybe he's my boss. For a very short period of time."

"Did you hear the one about the two old ladies sitting on the front porch?"

"Spare me."

"What? You can have it. It's free. Use it in your act."

"I don't tell jokes," I said, my voice its usual frosty tone when dealing with civilians stepping into my domain.

Detective Pucci snorted. "So what do you do if you don't tell jokes?"

"I have a comedy routine. It's not just jokes. It's body language and facial expression and timing. Lots and lots of timing."

"So you wanna hear this joke or not?" he said, opening the door of Bert's office and ushering me in.

I threw myself down on the couch. "Get it over with."

He sat down in the chair behind Bert's desk.

"Okay, so these two old ladies are sitting on the porch. One of 'em says, 'Oh, shit,'—excuse me."

"Go right ahead."

" 'Oh, shit, here comes my husband with a dozen roses. Now I'll have to spend twelve hours on my back.' The other lady says, 'What? You don't have a vase?' "

Detective Pucci laughed until he looked at me. Then he sobered. "Okay, so about last night," he said.

"What about it?"

"When did Mr. Neusberg arrive at your place?"

"It was after one o'clock."

"You two were an item, huh?"

"We've known each other for a while."

He scratched his two-hour-early five-o'clock shadow. "You wanna tell me what exactly happened?"

"Not particularly."

He raised an eyebrow. My mother can do that. Every time she did that to me as a child, I confessed everything I'd done that week. I had a sort of Pavlovian response to Pucci's raised eyebrow. I told him everything that had happened from the green room until I called the desk.

"This must be very difficult for you, Ms. Kruse," he said.

"It ain't a piece a cake, Detective."

"Did the two of you have drinks before . . . well . . ."

"Before we started humping each other's brains out? No. We just got right to it."

"No drinks? No water? No snacks? Chips, anything like that?" he asked.

"I told you, no. . . ."

"How about in the green room earlier? Did you see Mr. Neusberg ingest anything?"

My numb brain began to awaken. "Food poisoning? Is that what happened?"

"I'm not at liberty to give any details at this time, Ms. Kruse. We're still in the investigative stage."

"Look, I think I have a vested interest in this. If he had something . . . some disease . . . well, I think I have a right to know," I said.

"The ME doesn't believe it was a disease, Ms. Kruse."

"Then you think it was an accident, like food poisoning?"

"As I said, Ms. Kruse, I'm not at liberty to—"

"Oh, come on!"

He raised that eyebrow again. I vaguely wondered if, because my mother did this so dramatically, it was an Oedipal thing to find a man who could raise one eyebrow attractive. Not that I found Pucci attractive. In the least.

He stood up from Bert's desk chair and walked to the door, opening it and holding it for me. "You can go back to the green room or back to your hotel. You're free to go wherever you want, Ms. Kruse. As long as you don't leave town."

I looked at him, my eyes wide. I've watched enough TV in cheap hotel rooms to know that "don't leave town" meant only one thing. Foul play.

"Oh, Lord," I said. "He was murdered."

"I beg your pardon?" Pucci said. Neither eyebrow was raised. Actually they were both lowered, frowning hard at me. He pushed me back into the office and closed the door.

"Nothing," I said, trying to get around him to the doorknob.

"Don't repeat that to anyone right now, Ms. Kruse. Do you understand?"

I bristled at his tone. "Is that an order, Detective Gucci?"

"Pucci. And yes, Ms. Kruse, it is."

I moved around him and opened the door, going into the hall and heading back to the green room, only because I'd left my purse in there. Which is a dumb thing to do around comedians, as poorly as we're paid.

I could hear conversations going full blast in the green room as I approached. They stopped—excuse the expression—dead as soon as I walked into the room.

I went quickly to the chair where I'd been sitting and picked up my purse.

"Well? Did you tell *him* what happened?" Bucky Schwartz asked.

"Bucky!" Babe scolded. "Stop."

"Yes, Bucky, if you want to talk, why don't we do it in the office?" Detective Pucci said behind me. I hadn't known he'd been following me. One part of my brain wondered if he'd been watching my butt as I walked down the hall. The other part wondered if he'd been considering how I'd look in prison garb.

Detective Pucci held the door open for both Bucky and me. Only I turned right, toward the back door, while they turned left.

Over his shoulder, Pucci said, "If you decide to change hotels, Ms. Kruse, let us know."

"Certainly, Detective Lucci."

"Pucci," he said.

threw myself down on the bed and picked up the
phone, dialling Phoebe's office number.

"Anders and Love," the receptionist said.

"Luci, hi, it's me, Kimmey."

"Oh, Kimmey, I'm so sorry. Phoebe told me
what happened."

"Yeah. It's been pretty awful. Is she there?"

"Hold on," Luci said and put me on hold. A vio-
lin version of a Village People tune played in my ear
while I waited.

In a few seconds, Phoebe picked up. "Hey,
kiddo," she said.

"I think I'm in trouble."

"What?" she said. "Still knocking 'em dead?"

"You're sick," I said.

"Sorry. What's up?" I could hear her thousand-dollar leather office chair settle with the weight of her body.

"I may need your services."

"You planning on merging with a conglomerate?"

"No, I'm afraid the plan is to merge me with the Illinois prison system."

"Spit it out, Kimmey."

I took a deep breath. "I think the police think that maybe . . ."

"You sure you're being evasive enough?"

". . . that maybe Cab was murdered," I said in one quick breath.

Phoebe was silent for a moment. "Interesting. And you're a suspect?"

"The number one suspect."

"You need a criminal attorney, hon, not a corporate one."

"I want you," I said.

"Only if you want to incorporate. Not if you want to stay out of prison." I could hear her Rolodex spinning. "Look. Let me find somebody to refer me to somebody in Chicago. Okay?"

"Phoebe!" I was close to tears.

"I know, I know." Phoebe sighed. "Well, they're all idiots up there if they think you could hurt a fly."

"Would you come tell 'em that, please?"

"You've got no motive," she said.

"He didn't call for three years," I supplied.

"Yeah, and I guess you had more opportunity than anybody else."

"Thanks."

"Means?" Phoebe asked.

"I have no idea."

"Has anybody said anything to you to indicate they plan to arrest you?" Phoebe asked, her lawyer hat obviously well positioned.

"The detective said for me not to leave town."

"Oh."

"Is that bad?" I asked.

"That ain't good. But he's probably telling everybody that. Can you find out if he told everyone that?"

"I can try."

"Okay. You do that. And I'll find an attorney in Chicago."

"A good one," I suggested.

"Yeah. A Yankee Racehorse Haynes."

"Now you're talking."

"Kimmey . . ."

"Yeah?"

Phoebe sighed. "Stay out of trouble, okay?"

"Why didn't you tell me that two days ago?"

I hung up and sat on the bed staring at the ceiling. Stay out of trouble, she said. That obviously meant don't leave the hotel room. I looked around my new surroundings. The same chenille bedspread, the same love seat in the same awful print, the same picture over the bed, except these big-eyed children were holding a big-eyed dog. My fingers played over the bald spots on the chenille spread, my mind obsessed with my predicament. I stood up finally and went into the bathroom and did some hand laundry. Straightened my makeup kit, putting everything in alphabetical order, then rearranging them in order of use. I went to the closet and sorted my wardrobe by type: blouses together, pants together, skirts together, the one dress standing by itself.

I spied my purse on the bed where I'd dropped it. I hadn't cleaned it out in about a month. I sat down cross-legged on the bed and dumped the contents of my purse on the spread. Purse-sized makeup kit, okay; purse-sized hair spray, okay; wallet, okay; checkbook, okay; a bottle of aspirin, okay; my airline ticket, okay; my little notebook where I keep expenses for the IRS, along with a paper clip for receipts, okay; an empty gum wrapper, trash; my receipt for lunch, stick in paper clip; my taxi receipt, paper clip; a grocery list from three weeks ago, trash; a bottle of Lanoxin, okay . . .

No. I looked at the bottle. The top part of the prescription label was torn off. The part that said the name of the drugstore, the number, and the names of the prescriptee and the doctor. All that was left was *Lanoxin, 1.25 mg.*

I dropped it on the bed like it was on fire. A strange prescription bottle in my purse. In my purse that had been left for fifteen to twenty minutes in the green room while I was wasting time with Detective Pucci. Oh, shit. I jumped up and stared at the bottle. I walked around the bed and stared at it from another angle. I went into the bathroom, rinsed my face, and came back out. The bottle still sat on the bed. And I still stared at it.

Okay, I told myself, options. Option one: Throw it away. Wipe it clear of fingerprints and throw it away. But would I be wiping away only my fingerprints? Okay, option two: Take it to Pucci. Tell him the truth.

I picked up my purse-sized makeup bag and

emptied the contents on the bed, scooting the prescription bottle inside without touching it.

Then I picked up the phone and dialed Phoebe's office number again.

"She's in conference, Kimmey," Luci said.

"Luce, it's an emergency."

"Well . . ."

"A really serious life-or-death-type emergency."

"Well . . . okay. Hold on." I listened to an orchestrated version of "Like a Virgin" until Phoebe came on the line.

"Kimmey, I said I'd get back to you. We're trying to negotiate a multimillion—"

"I found a prescription bottle in my purse."

"What?"

"Label torn mostly off. I don't know what it is. It says Lanoxin. What is that?"

"I'm a lawyer, not a doctor."

"What should I do?"

"Calm down."

I sat down on the bed, as far away from the purse-sized makeup bag with the prescription bottle as I could get. "Okay. I'm calm."

"You have to take it to the police," Phoebe said.

"Oh, Lord."

"You have to."

"With or without a lawyer?"

"Hold on."

I listened to the rest of "Like a Virgin" and the beginning of "Yesterday" before Phoebe came back on the line.

"Bernard Hazlet."

"I beg your pardon?"

"He's the Racehorse Haynes of Chicago. Here's his number." She read the digits with the Chicago area code. "Marty, my contact here, is calling him now. By the time you call, he should be expecting you."

"Thank you, Phoebe. Thank you, thank you."

"As soon as this is over, you get your butt back home, you hear?"

"Yes, ma'am."

I hung up and stared at the piece of paper with Hazlet's telephone number, then picked up the receiver and dialed.

"Ms. Kruse," he said, sticking out his hand.

"Detective Ducci," I said, shaking it.

"Pucci." He turned to Bernard Hazlet. "Mr. Hazlet. Nice to see you again."

"Detective." Hazlet and I both sat down in the chairs by Detective Pucci's desk, most of which was covered by an IBM-clone PC. Papers were scattered over the remaining area, and an in-out tray was bursting forth with more wood pulp. A picture by his computer showed the likenesses of two adolescent boys with receding hairlines and five-o'clock shadows. Obviously his sons. There was no picture of wife and mother to be seen from my vantage point.

Bernard Hazlet took a small tape recorder out of his pocket and placed it on the desk. "Do you mind if I record this, Detective?" he asked.

"Of course not, Mr. Hazlet." Pucci smiled. It was an awesome thing. Lots of white teeth and a dimple—in his chin. It wasn't there when he wasn't smiling. Odd, but I didn't know the human face could do that.

"It is April 13," Hazlet said into the recorder. "We are at the desk of Detective Sal Pucci of the Fourth Precinct, Chicago PD. Present are myself, Detective Pucci, and Ms. Kimberly Kruse.

"As you may be aware, Detective, my client left her purse in the green room while she had her meeting with you at the Kaiser Komedy Klub."

"No, I wasn't aware of that," Pucci said.

"You saw me pick it up when you came in to get Bucky Schwartz!" I said.

He looked at me. "Oh, yes. Is that what you were doing in there?"

"Later this afternoon, while cleaning out her purse, Ms. Kruse found a strange prescription drug bottle that does not belong to her. Since Mr. Neusberg possibly died under strange circumstances, we thought it best to bring it to you."

Hazlet held out his hand. I handed him the purse-sized makeup bag. He handed the makeup bag to Pucci. Pucci opened it and dropped the prescription bottle onto his desk.

"Well," he said, turning it around and around with a number two pencil.

"I picked it up when I first found it," I said, "so my fingerprints will be on it."

Pucci raised that eyebrow at me.

"It would be the normal thing to do, Detective," Hazlet said.

Pucci picked up the phone and dialed three digits and waited a minute. Then he said, "Doc, Lanoxin?" He listened for a few minutes, said, "Thanks," and hung up.

He looked at me and then at Hazlet. "Lanoxin is a brand name for the generic drug digitalis. Digitalis is used for the control of certain heart conditions. This particular brand is slow release. As I understand it, as explained to me just now by the ME's office, digitalis given to a person who does *not* have a heart condition can cause certain problems. An overdose of digitalis given to a person who does *not* have a heart condition can cause cardiac arrhythmia."

"Why are you telling us this, Detective?" Hazlet asked.

"Because Cab Neusberg had enough digitalis in his system to kill a Buick with heart disease."

I stood in the wings watching Joey Scarlotti. What did I know about him? Nothing. Did he know Cab? Had they worked together before? Did Cab steal a girl or a gig from him? What was Joey's motive? I knew I should've been thinking about my routine, polishing and perfecting, but I couldn't remember it. Not a word of it. I stood there, on deck, the next to go on, and I couldn't remember a word of my routine.

Joey finished to mediocre applause. The house was half empty. Bert said people had been demanding their money back all day. They'd paid to see Cab Neusberg. Not Joey Scarlotti or Bobby Rivers or Babe Marsh or Kimmey Kruse.

Joey Scarlotti came past me, holding his throat with both hands and mugging strangulation.

"Très amusant," I said as haughtily as I could muster.

He giggled and went on by. Mickey Reynolds

was on stage telling his joke. A drunk in the back laughed. Then Mickey introduced me. The applause was not enough to lift my spirits and reunite my head with my routine. I went out on stage and took the microphone in my hand.

For want of anything better to pop up, I said, "A bear goes into a bar for a beer . . ."

I went into the green room and threw myself on the couch. As I lay there, I thought, I've been bad before, I've laid an egg, bombed, done all those things, sometimes simultaneously, but I've never gone out on stage before and told a *joke*.

Babe Marsh had commandeered the love seat. She leaned over to me and patted my leg. "You were very funny tonight, Kimmey," she said, smiling, a muscle contraction that turned her double chin into a quadruple chin and caused rolls of fat to make her eyes disappear.

I've never had much respect for overweight comedians who tell fat jokes. One of the reasons John Candy's always been a hero of mine. Fat jokes are easy and cheap and I've never heard John tell one. He's a big guy who's funny. Period. Babe, on the other hand, had no other material in her repertoire.

"I was awful," I answered.

"Oh, no," Babe said, frowning, her hand shaking my leg, which also shook the flab that hung down from her upper arm. "You were just wonderful. You always are." She sighed and sat back on her love seat. "And you're so little and cute. It must be great."

Instantly I felt like an ass for the things I'd been

thinking. She probably had medical problems, an underactive thyroid or bad glands or something that caused the weight problem.

"Try reaching the top shelf of something," I said.

Babe laughed. "What you need is one of those collapsible stools to carry in your purse."

My purse. Interesting thought. "Speaking of my purse," I said, sitting up and turning to Babe, "did you notice anyone messing with it while I was in talking with that detective earlier?"

"Oh, goodness, is something missing?"

"Well, I think so, but I'm not sure," I lied. "I can't find . . . my mother's brooch. I'm pretty sure I put it in my purse."

"Well, gosh, Kimmey, I sure didn't notice. I'm sorry."

"Was anybody up moving around while I was gone?"

Babe looked at the ceiling for guidance. "Well, now, I'm not sure." She lowered her head and smiled at me. "I wasn't really paying attention." She shrugged her massive shoulders. Then her piggy eyes got large. "Oh, wait. That woman—the one who came in with Cab last night?"

"The agent/manager type?"

"Right. Well, she was talking the whole time on that cellular phone and she was moving around the whole time. Touching things."

"Touching things? What things?" I sat up straight. Now we were getting somewhere.

"Oh, you know, straightening a picture, rearranging the magazines on the coffee table. I didn't see her go near your purse, though. Of course, I wasn't really watching her that much." Babe leaned forward to whisper. "She sorta intimidates me."

I patted her massive arm. "Don't let that type intimidate you. They're usually all show and no go, as my daddy's fond of saying."

Babe giggled. "Oh, I just love it when you talk that Texas stuff." Again, she sighed. "I'm from Ohio. There's nothing funny about Ohio." She frowned in thought. "Except, of course, for Cleveland. And I never understood why people think that's funny."

"I guess it all started with the river catching on fire," I said, lying back down in an attempt to end the conversation.

"Oh, but that wasn't funny! That was awful! All that pollution!"

I nodded my head. "Yeah, I guess it was, really. But nothing's sacred to a comic."

Remembering my next investigative move, I looked up into the piggy eyes. "Did you have an interview with Detective Pucci?"

Babe nodded. "Yes. Very interesting. He seems like a nice person."

I snorted. "I'll try to remember that when he's testifying against me in a court of law."

Babe moved her bulk toward me and patted my arm. "Oh, Kimmey, don't be silly! He knows you had nothing to do with it!"

"Did he tell you not to leave town?"

Babe thought for a minute. "Well, you know, as a matter of fact, I think he did." Her eyes got wide. "Oh, goodness." She giggled again. "Do you think he suspects *me?*"

I closed my eyes in relief. Okay, so I wasn't the only person who wasn't supposed to "leave town."

I put my arm over my eyes and we both sat there silently for a few minutes. Then Babe said, "I was real sorry to hear about Cab. It must have been awful for you."

"Yeah. Thanks. It was pretty bad, all right."

"He was such a nice person."

I opened my eyes and looked at Babe. Babe? Did she have a crush on him? Did Cab rebuff her? Maybe he made a crack and she took offense? Was I going to look at everyone I knew and wonder if they'd killed Cab Neusberg? No, just the ones that were around last night. And Babe had been around.

The door opened and I closed my eyes again. If it was Bobby or Joey I'd just as soon they thought I was asleep. Then maybe they wouldn't talk to me. Or about me.

"Ms. Kruse?"

I looked up into the dark, brooding eyes of Detective Pucci. I sat up. "Oh, hi, Detective Tucci," I said.

"Pucci," he said.

The door opened again and Mickey Reynolds stuck his head in. "Babe, you're on deck."

Babe pushed herself to her feet and smiled at Detective Pucci and me. "Well, here goes nothing," she said, waddling to the door.

We were in a different order tonight, each of us doing a longer bit to take up the slack of a dead headliner.

After the door closed, Detective Pucci sat down

on the love seat across from me. "We've got a problem," he said.

I braced myself. "What's that?"

"Yours are the only fingerprints on the prescription bottle."

I could feel a knot growing in the tendons in the back of my neck. My palms were clammy and my throat was dry. I was either in love or in very deep shit. "I told you I'd touched the bottle."

Pucci nodded. "Yeah. You told me that."

"I could have thrown the damn thing away!"

Pucci settled back in the love seat. "Why didn't you?"

"Because I'm a law-abiding citizen!"

He pulled a notebook out of his inside jacket pocket and flipped it open. "Is that why you were busted for possession of marijuana in nineteen eighty-four?"

I threw myself back down on the couch, covering my eyes with my arm. "Oh, hell." I lifted the arm and looked at Detective Pucci. "It was two roaches in the ashtray of my car and they weren't even mine. The judge reprimanded me and released me on my own recognizance."

The dark eyes moved from me to the notebook. "And the DWI in nineteen eighty-six?"

I sat up. "That wasn't a DWI! That was supposed to be removed from my record!"

He flourished the notepad at me. "Not so I've noticed."

"I wasn't drunk! I hadn't even been drinking!" It was Phoebe and me in the car, two-thirty A.M., coming back from her folks' house in the hills to our apartment by the university. We had a severe case of the giggling simples. I was driving. I weaved from one lane to another because I was laughing so hard there were tears in my eyes. When the cop pulled me over, I couldn't walk a straight line. But I demanded a Breathalyzer test. And I'd passed. I told Pucci that. That I'd passed the Breathalyzer. How could I explain the giggling simples to a Chicago cop?

Again, his eyes moved from me to the notebook. "Indecent exposure?"

I sighed. "A bunch of us in college went skinny-dipping in Lake Austin. An old prude with no sense of humor called the cops—I mean, the police. We paid a fine." I was getting mad. I'm stupid when I'm mad. "What? You didn't find the four murders by poison and the three strangulations? What about that guy I boiled in oil because he wouldn't put out?"

Pucci flipped the notebook shut and stuck it back in his inside jacket pocket. He grinned at me. "Missed those, I guess."

"And you call yourself a public servant."

"Actually, I don't. I call myself the Italian Stallion."

Raising one eyebrow would have come in handy at that moment, but all I could muster was a sneer. "You could be arrested for false advertising," I said.

"According to the law, the product has to be checked for failure to perform first."

I sat back on the couch, pulling my knees up and hugging them to my body. "Are you flirting with me, Detective?"

"Of course not," he said. "It would be unseemly

for an investigative officer to flirt with his number one murder suspect."

My stomach heaved. I'd rather he was flirting. "I'm your number one suspect?" I noticed my voice was about five octaves higher than my Kathleen Turner imitation.

He shrugged. "Everybody's a suspect right now, Ms. Kruse." He stood up. "Can I give you a ride back to your hotel?" he asked.

I shook my head. "No, that's okay." Pucci nodded his head and walked out of the green room. I didn't tell him I'd rather walk on the off chance I might get mugged and brighten my day.

4

I lay in bed at the hotel and stared at the ceiling. It had an uncanny resemblance to the ceiling that had been above me during the five minutes or so I'd been making love to Cab. The tears came and I rolled over on my side, remembering the title to my father's favorite country and western tune, "I Got Tears in My Ears from Lyin' on My Back Crying over You."

I looked at the clock. Three-thirty. I rolled out of bed, put on my robe and slippers, and slipped out of my room and down the hall to the Coke machine. If I was going to be awake all night, I might as well go for the caffeine-and-sugar rush.

I got back to my room, sat down on the bed, and popped the top and took a giant swallow. And thought about Cab. He was a cute, sweet, sexy guy.

And I'd liked him a lot. I didn't love him, though. I knew that. It's hard to love someone who thinks of you as nothing but a nice but very occasional roll in the hay.

He was my usual BMOC crush. I found them wherever I went. In high school, it was Buddy Kincaide, the quarterback of the football team. Whenever he spoke to me, which wasn't often, he called me Tammy. It wasn't a cute nickname. He just got it confused with Kimmey.

In college my BMOCs changed each semester, until Billy came along. Before him, the crushes were on the leader of the anti-apartheid movement, the president of the student association at Dobie Tower, a guitar player at a club on the drag, and the head waiter at Tracy's sorority house. BMOC is all relative. Of course, my marriage to David was actually snagging the BMOC. What's BMOCer than your boss, right? And then there was Cab. The headliner. The guy who actually did Letterman *and* Carson. Twice on Arsenio. And there was a rumor he was asked to do an HBO "One Night Stand" but something fell through. Everyone tries to start that rumor about themselves, though.

But, and this is a big but, he was the first BMOC to drop dead on top of me. I suppose, in the great scheme of things, that will make him memorable.

Of course, I thought, if I end up in prison accused of his murder, it would be hard to get him off my mind. Then I realized that if I went to prison, the last heterosexual sex I might ever have would have been five minutes long and not particularly good.

I put the Coke on the bedside table, threw myself across the bed, and tried to sob, but nothing would come. So I sat up again. I wasn't going to prison, I told myself. I don't look good in drab. And I don't want a boyfriend named Roxanne.

Pucci was looking at me for this. Looking at me hard. Hadn't he pulled up my rap sheet? Such as it was? I mean, to get all bent out of shape by a very minor possession charge, a DWI that hadn't been, and a stupid indecent exposure? That means I'm a murderer?

Somebody at the Kaiser Komedy Klub had killed Cab Neusberg. More than likely. And somebody at the Kaiser Komedy Klub had tried to frame me for it by putting the prescription bottle of Lanoxin in my purse. I had to hope it was one of them, because if it wasn't, then it could be anybody and I couldn't see just anybody being able to walk into the green room and mess around with my purse. My best bet would be to concentrate on those there that night. What did I know about them?

I got out a pad of paper and a pen and began writing:

Babe Marsh—from Ohio. Town? Relationship to Cab?

Joey Scarlotti—from New York City. Had he ever worked with Cab? Find out.

Bobby Rivers—from some town in southern California. What was his relationship to Cab? Find out.

Bucky Schwartz—from? Relationship to Cab: Employee. Gofer. How did he really feel about him? Feel him out.

*Mickey Reynolds—? Know nothing at all about
Mickey! Find out!*

*Bert Kaiser—Did Cab have money in the Klub?
Interesting. Find out. Find out any other connection.
Did they know each other before?*

*Agent/Manager—???? Mystery woman. Find out at
least her name, stupid!*

Finally feeling as though I'd accomplished
something, I put the paper down on the bedside
table and went to sleep.

At ten o'clock the next morning, I was at the Kaiser
Komedy Klub. I knocked on the back door and an
old black man with a broom opened it.

"Hi, I'm Kimmey Kruse."

"Yes'm, you one of them comics, right?"

"Yes, sir. Is Mr. Kaiser in?"

"Yes'm, he in his office." He pointed an arthritic
finger down the long, dark hallway. "Back thata-
way."

I thanked him and headed down the hall. As I
neared the door to Bert's office, I could hear a one-
sided conversation—Bert was obviously on the
phone. I stopped.

"It's been taken care of!" Bert said. "I said I'd do
it and I did it! What? You think I'm stupid? Nobody
knows nothing." There was a silence, then Bert
said, "Don't threaten me! Don't do it! I'll bring you
down you threaten me! You're in this up to your
turkey-wattle neck!"

"Right there, ma'am. That his office," the old
man said.

I smiled. "Thank you," I said, and walked to the doorway of Bert's office. He had his hand over the receiver, obviously having heard the old man and me.

He smiled big, flashing his perfect false teeth. "Kimmey! Kid, how you doing? Come in, come in!" He waved his hand at his couch. "Sit! Give me a sec." Back to the phone he said, "I'll have to get back to you. Yeah. Later." He hung up, turned to me, full-voltage smile once again in place. "Ya did good last night, kid, under the circumstances."

Whoa, I thought, low blow.

"You okay for tonight?" Bert asked.

I nodded.

He shuffled some papers on his desk. "Not that it matters. The house'll be emptier than temple on Good Friday. Been getting cancellations all damn morning."

"I'm sorry to hear that," I said.

Bert slowly shook his head. "It ain't been good, kid, it ain't been good."

"Well, Cab's certainly going to be missed."

"Now, that's the truth," Bert said, leaning forward on his desk, giving me his sincere look. The one club owners give you when they tell you the check's in the mail. Which is remarkably close to the look they give you when they say, "Kid, I loved your act. My people love your act. It's the audiences we're getting. They're not, ya know, sophisticated," which is said right before they fire you.

"Did you know him long?" I asked. Innocently.

Bert leaned back in his chair and waved his hand in the air. "I gave the kid his first break. Back at Lou's on the Lake in Tahoe. Funny guy. Fun-*ny* guy!" He shook his head at the sadness of it all. "He's gonna be missed, kiddo. Like you said, he's gonna be missed."

"You must have been good friends," I suggested.

"He was like a son to me. A *son!*" He shook his head again. Then he met my eyes. "I know this has gotta be rough on you kid, and I'm really sorry."

I nodded my head. "It wasn't the greatest experience in the world."

"Yeah," Bert said, "me too. First time I ever had a headliner die on me." He looked away, then looked back and said, "Oops."

I got up and Bert stood too. He was of the old school. "Well, I just came by to see if we were still on tonight," I said. "And to get out of my hotel!" I laughed. He laughed. We both laughed. I walked to the door. "See you tonight," I said, waving a hand behind me as I left the office.

I got back to the hotel in time for lunch. Today, along with my usual double-meat cheeseburger, fries, onion rings, and a strawberry malt, I decided to have a salad. With Thousand Island dressing. To keep down the health-code violations.

Max brought me my food. "You hear about the insomniac agnostic with dyslexia?" he asked.

I groaned. "No, but I'm afraid I'm going to."

"Sometimes he wakes up in the middle of the night and wonders if there *is* a dog."

"You know how many women with PMS it takes to change a light bulb?"

Max and I both turned at the new voice. Pucci. Standing there in *my* hotel dining room.

Max grinned. "No. How many?"

"What's it to you, asshole?"

Max laughed all the way back to the kitchen. Pucci grinned as he sat down. "Ms. Kruse."

"Detective Nucci."

"Pucci."

We stared at each other. Finally, he cleared his throat and said, "So this is where you stay when you're in town?" He looked around the dining room of the Lake House; at its rippled linoleum, its mismatched dinette chairs with tape over the holes so the stuffing wouldn't come out, at the chipped tables, and paint-wanting walls.

"I know the owners," I said.

He nodded. "So. How you doing?"

I shrugged. "Fine. How are you?"

"Fine."

We sat there staring at the rippled linoleum, mismatched dinette chairs, chipped tables, and paint-wanting walls.

Finally, not being able to stand it much longer, I said, "Detective, why are you here?"

"Just checking to make sure you are where you say you are. We do that with all our suspects."

"Must keep you busy."

Pucci shrugged. "I've had uniforms check on everybody else."

"Why am I getting the honor of your presence?"

He grinned. I didn't like the look of it. I could see him using the same grin in a courtroom while they dragged away someone he'd just testified against. Like me, maybe. "Just worked out that way," was his lame excuse.

I looked at the cheeseburger fat congealing on my plate. I was losing my appetite. The last time I did that I had appendicitis—when I was twelve years old. Did I dare tell him of the telephone conversation I overheard at the comedy club? Or should I keep that to myself? I wasn't sure how much digging Pucci was willing to do on other people, not when he had me to throw in jail.

"Did you know Bert Kaiser's known Cab for years?" I said. "Claims to have started him in the business."

"Yeah, I knew that," Pucci said.

"Did you know that I *think* Babe Marsh knew him before, too?"

"Yeah, I also know that. They worked together about six months ago in Atlanta. He also worked with Joey Scarlotti and covered for Bobby Rivers on the Arsenio Hall show about six weeks ago."

"Covered for him?" I asked, frowning. "What does that mean?"

Pucci shrugged. "Rivers said something came up and he couldn't make the show and Cab covered for him."

I snorted. "Bull. Bobby Rivers would give up his left nut before he'd give up Arsenio!"

Pucci shrugged again. "I'm just repeating what I was told."

"By who?"

Pucci grinned. "Whom."

I waved my hand, dislodging his correction of my grammar and sending it flying around the room. "Whatever. Whom?"

"Rivers," he said. "When I interviewed him yesterday."

I pushed myself away from the table. It was obvious I wasn't going to eat any time soon. Not with Pucci in the room. "I still say it's bull. Give me a minute."

I walked over to the counter, Pucci right behind me, and asked Max if I could use the phone. He handed up a white princess from a ledge below the counter and I dialed my long-distance code and then my agent's number.

"Myra Mitchell's office," a hard-core New York accent stated.

"Myra, please. Kimmey Kruse calling."

"Yeah, okay. Just a minute."

I was put on hold. Pucci raised that eyebrow. At this point, I was wondering how effective a steak knife would be removing it. "My agent," I answered his nonverbal question. "She's a friend of somebody on Arsenio."

"So why haven't you ever been—"

"Myra," I said, turning away from Pucci and concentrating on the telephone in my hand.

"Kimmey! God! I was just going to call you! It's terrible about Cab Neusberg! My God, were you there?"

Closer than you'd think, I thought, but didn't say. "Yeah, Myra, it was pretty awful."

"Any idea who—"

"That's why I'm calling," I interrupted, "if you can keep this strictly confidential . . ."

"My lips are sealed. Like glue."

"Could you call that friend of yours who works with Arsenio and find out what happened about six weeks ago? Bobby Rivers was supposed to have a gig but instead they went with Cab. I wanna know what *really* happened."

"You want the skinny, honey, you came to the right place. You still at that nasty hotel?"

"Yep."

"I'll call you back in fifteen."

With that, the line went dead.

"She's going to call me back in my room."

Pucci held out his arm. "Madam," he said.

I'd glanced through every bit of reading material I had, stared out the window, memorizing the lay of the building across the alley, given minimal answers to every query and grunts to all opinions voiced by Detective Pucci, until finally the phone rang.

I grabbed it like a bargain at Neiman Marcus and put the receiver to my ear. "Hello?"

"Kimmey?" Myra said. "Boy, have I got some skinny."

"Hold on. The police detective who's handling the case is here with me. I want him to hear this, too."

Pucci came over and stuck his ear close to mine. I could feel the beginnings of his early five-o'clock shadow and smell his aftershave. Something simple and rustic, like Old Spice or Aqua Velva.

"Go ahead," I said.

"Okay. Cab and Bobby have the same agent, Abel Axelrod. Abel got Bobby the gig with Arsenio. Then at the last minute he called them and asked if they'd mind a switch. Seems Cab had some new material he wanted to try out. Naturally, Arsenio's people said fine, Cab being a much bigger pull than

Bobby. As far as I can tell, Abel just axed Bobby and put Cab in his place. Not the kind of thing I'd do with any of *my* talent."

Right, I thought. Unless there was a buck in it. I looked at Pucci. "Any questions?"

He took the phone from my hand. "Can I have the name and number of the person you got that information from?" he asked, pulling the nasty little notebook with my transgressions in it from his jacket pocket. He scribbled down the information. "Now, you got a number for this Abel guy?"

"Abel Axelrod," I said aloud. I'd been thinking about switching to him. He seemed to get his people a lot more action than Myra ever got me. I mean, Bobby *almost* made Arsenio. The closest I've gotten is my TV set.

Pucci wrote down that information, too, in his little notebook, thanked Myra, and hung up.

"You got good instincts," he said to me.

"Well, nobody at Bobby's level doesn't do Arsenio because they have a headache or their mother died."

Pucci was staring at me. I looked away. "Well," I said, "I guess . . ."

"Do you wanna sleep with me?"

I turned to Pucci. He was lounging on my bed like he owned the place.

"What? You got a death wish?"

He grinned. "Real men always like to live on the edge."

"You want to sleep with your number one suspect?"

He sat up. "You're not my number one suspect." He shrugged. "The rest of the department's pretty sure about you, and so's the DA, but not me."

If you've never had the feeling of your stomach sinking and your heart rising simultaneously, let me tell you, it's not up there on the list with orgasms, sneezes, and a good bowel movement.

"Why do you not consider me a suspect?" I asked. I had no desire to know why everyone else thought I was.

"I didn't say I didn't consider you a suspect," Pucci said, "just not my number one suspect. Mainly, because I think you're too smart to time a murder where you'd be . . . ah . . . so much in the vicinity, so to speak. Also, I don't think you're clever enough to have worked it out that I would think what I just said so do it anyway. If you know what I mean."

My whole body bristled. "Not clever enough?" I grabbed my purse and opened my wallet, pulling out the review I always carried. The one from the *Buffalo Evening News*. I read it out loud. "Kimmey Kruse is an amusing, *clever* comedian well worth the price of admission'!"

Again, he lay back on the bed, lounging on his side, one arm holding up his head. Sort of like the antique Burt Reynolds centerfold in *Playgirl*. He grinned at me. "Okay. Clever's not the right word. Let's say cunning."

I put the clipping back in my billfold. I nodded. "Okay. I'll buy cunning."

"So, anyway," Pucci said, "you wanna sleep with me?"

I got up from the chair I'd been sitting on and

walked to the door, holding it wide for him. "No, Detective Zucci, I don't."

Pucci stood up and walked past me to the door. "Pucci," he said, and kept walking.

5

And then he says, 'You wanna sleep with me'!"
I could hear Phoebe shaking her short
blond hair over the telephone. Well, maybe
not exactly hear it, but I knew that's what she was
doing. "That's sick."

"Tell me about it!"

"So. Do you wanna?"

"Phoebe . . ."

"You've slept with worse."

"Why do I call you? Why do I put myself
through this torture?"

"Because we're sisters and you have to."

She was right. Although we were both only
children born to different sets of parents, we'd
taken a blood oath and become sisters in the eighth
grade. We called each other's parents Mom-two
and Daddy-two. We'd lived together as roommates

since our freshman year at UT, excluding the three years I was living with Bobby and the nine months I was married to David. And, of course, the year and a half she was living with Nathaniel, the creep she married. They were still legally married, even though they hadn't seen each other in two years. The house Phoebe lived in, a great old Texas Gothic, was bought while they were together. The down payment was made with her money and the monthly mortgage was always met with her money, but he liked to think of it as community property. Although they paid little for it when they first got it, with inflation and the crazy Austin economy, the property was now worth a quarter of a million. So Phoebe had refused to divorce him. Very good strategy on her part. Unless she met somebody else.

Phoebe and I had spoken to each other every day of our lives since the seventh grade. Which was the reason I had a monthly phone bill larger than most people's home mortgages. When I was at home, Austin, I lived in a garage apartment in Phoebe's backyard. When I was on the road, I called. Just like she did every day of the three weeks she was in Europe two years ago. Just like I did every day at summer camp when our parents decided to separate us because they thought we were getting "too close." A parental euphemism for, "Oh, my God, do you think our daughters are lesbians?" Our parents may have been the only parents in history to sigh in collective relief upon discovering our losses of virginity.

"He's a creep," I said.

"Definitely. To say something like that." I could hear a noise on the other end of the line.

"What are you doing?"

"Putting Sara in the microwave."

"Phoebe!"

She sighed. "I'll only eat half." Phoebe was a Sara Lee junkie. Her specialty was Sara Lee pecan coffee cake, although she'd eat just about anything with the red-and-white label on it. When I mentioned I had to work to gain weight and most women I know hate me for it, the main woman it got to was Phoebe. She'd fought a weight problem all her life. Nothing major. No Babe Marsh-type problem. Just a steady twenty to thirty pounds overweight. When we were kids, she insisted on wearing a T-shirt and shorts over her swimsuit when she went swimming. She'd gone on every kind of diet anyone's ever come up with. She'd lose five pounds and put ten back on.

"I thought you were Slim-Fasting," I said.

"Yeah, well the chocolate's great with doughnuts."

"Phoebe!"

"I'm kidding. Look, let's discuss something more positive than my weight problem. Like your impending arrest."

"Oh, Lord, do you think—"

"No, I don't. Have you talked to Hazlet lately?"

"If you don't think I'm going to be arrested, why do you think I need to keep in touch with Hazlet?"

She sighed. "I don't think you need to keep in touch with him. I just wondered."

"I'll call him right now."

"Kimmey. Don't call him right now. It's nine o'clock at night. Just touch base with him sometime tomorrow. Let him know what the detective said about the DA's office. Also, just for insurance, let him know Tucci propositioned you."

"Pucci." Damn, that got on my nerves. Phoebe always did that. Pick up on nicknames or whatever that I had going with some boy. In junior high, she did that with Winston Davis. I called him Pooh. You know, as in "Winnie the"? Then Phoebe started calling him that. Within a week, he was calling her Robin and they were a hot item in the lunchroom. "Why should I let him know Pucci propositioned me?" I asked.

"So we can sue later for sexual harassment if they ever arrest you. It would be a nice confusion to keep the jury's mind off the issue at hand."

I sighed and sank down deeper in the pillows. "They'd just think what Pucci obviously thought when he did it."

"What's that?"

"That if I'd sleep with a man who'd die on me, I'd sleep with anybody."

Phoebe laughed.

"It's not funny," I said. "Pucci obviously thinks I'm a slut! I don't like people, even people I don't like, thinking . . ."

"You like Gucci—"

"Pucci, and no, I don't like him. I loathe him. With every fiber of my being. But I still don't want him thinking I'm a slut! Because I'm not a slut." There was silence on the other end of the line. "Phoebe, am I a slut?"

"No, you're not a slut. You just have very poor taste in men."

"I'm not still married to a narcissistic philanderer named Nathaniel."

"What about that guy, Robert, who wrote bad checks and stole your wallet?"

"I never slept with him!"

"Moot point."

"What about that guy you dated right before you met Nathaniel?"

"Who?" Phoebe demanded.

"Brent or Bart or Bret or one of those names . . ."

"Brad."

"Right. Did he or did he not clip his toenails in the living room?" I demanded.

"All right," Phoebe said, warming up, "what about Tommy Dale?"

"Oh, Lord." I couldn't believe she would bring *that* up.

"Huh?" she demanded. "Tommy Dale. Tommy Dale, Tommy Dale."

"I didn't sleep with him."

"No, but you did go to a party with him. And even dated him *after* the party where he . . . now what was it?"

"Stop!" I cried.

"Seems to me he brought a . . . oh, gosh, how could I forget? What was it he brought to that party, Kimmey?"

"Phoebe . . ."

"Hum?"

I sighed. "A rubber chicken."

"And what did he do with that rubber chicken, Kimmey?"

Again I sighed. In a monotone, I recited, "He wore it on his head and said, 'Help me, help me, I have a rubber chicken on my head.' "

"And how many times did you go out with him after that?"

"Three."

"I rest my case. You have had more rotten men in your life than I have."

The phone rang at eight A.M. "Hello?" I said to the clock radio. After the third ring, I found the phone and picked it up. "Hello?"

"Ms. Kruse?"

I sank back in the pillows. "Yes."

"Pucci. Would you like to go with me to talk with Bobby Rivers?"

I sat up in bed. "I'll be ready in ten minutes."

"Fine, but I'll be there in thirty."

Mid-April in Chicago is not exactly mid-April in Austin, Texas. That morning in Austin, right that minute, birds were chirping, the azaleas were blooming, the fruit trees had gone from bloom to leaf, and suburbanites were gassing up their lawn mowers. In Chicago, the trees were still bare, grass was still brown, and the people had gone from their winter coats to their lightweight spring coats—a concept totally lost on a hill country Texan.

Pucci left the outskirts of the Old Town section, where the Lake House was, and headed south on Lakeshore toward downtown.

It was my first time in an unmarked police car. "Do you have a siren?"

"Yes."

"Do you have one of those red bubble lights like they use on TV?"

He pointed under the dash. I looked. There it was.

"Do you have a radio?"

He stopped at a red light and looked at me. "Do you want to talk on the radio and run the light and siren?"

I shrugged. "Only if necessary."

"It's not necessary."

"Oh." I sighed. "Okay, then." After a moment's silence, I asked, "Do you have a gun?"

He raised one side of his jacket to show a pistol riding on his hip. He began to move with the traffic, heading for the hotel near the Kaiser Komedy Klub where everybody except Cab Neusberg and me had rooms.

When a comic is working out of town, the club almost always provides lodging. Usually, it's a condo or apartment, something that looks like animals have been living there. The four-legged kind. There's usually a kitchen with no pans or utensils for eating, and furniture donated from the leftovers at garage sales. I once went out and bought an air mattress to sleep on because the bed I was given smelled like something had died on it and was covered with bloodstains. When a condo isn't provided, it's usually a hotel room in a dump that makes the Lake House look like the Plaza. That's why I stay with friends whenever possible and jump at the chance of staying at the Lake House while I'm in Chicago. How was I supposed to know that Bert Kaiser owned more than half of one of Chicago's nicest hotels—the Carlton—and had a floor of rooms at his disposal where he put his comics? By the time I found out about the Carlton, I'd already checked into the Lake House and didn't have the heart to tell Max and Tracy I'd rather stay uptown. I'm rude, but never tacky.

After a few moments of silence, Pucci pulled into the entryway of the hotel and parked the car. When the valet came to get the keys, Pucci flipped his badge at him and we walked in the hotel. I grinned to myself. It wasn't a bad way to get around the city.

Bobby Rivers was having breakfast in the main dining room. Instead of ripply linoleum they had a muted brown, beige, and black floral-patterned carpet. Instead of dinette chairs with tape covering holes in the padding, they had rattan chairs with large, plush cushions. Instead of chipped Formica tables, they had beveled glass tops over intricate rattan, with china and crystal and silver displayed on top. Instead of paint-wanting walls, they had silk-covered walls with framed paintings. Loyalty can be a pain in the ass.

"Hi, Kimmey," Bobby said, standing up partially and wiping his mouth with a linen napkin. He was wearing his usual attire—a Ralph Lauren pullover polo shirt, khaki Guess? jeans, and $200 pump-up running shoes. The perfect picture of the California Yuppie. "Detective Pucci."

He motioned for us to join him. Pucci held a chair for me and I tentatively sat down. For some reason, he reminded me of the guy in sixth grade who held the chair in the cafeteria for me and then, as I began to sit, pulled it all the way out. The guy in the sixth grade had a bad case of early five-o'clock shadow, too.

"Hope you don't mind if we join you," Pucci said.

"Not at all. What are you two doing out together this early in the morning?" His grin would follow me to the grave. Yes, Bobby, I sleep with anybody. How about you and me later in the Jacuzzi?

"Ms. Kruse agreed to accompany me this morning to speak with you about something. She's been very helpful on the case. As I hope you'll be."

Bobby sobered. "Of course. I'll help you any way I can."

A waiter came up and Pucci and I ordered coffee. I also ordered two eggs over easy, a small sirloin, hash browns, toast, and orange juice.

"I'd like to go over your statement of the other night." Pucci brought out the ever-present notebook, flipped to the right page, and went on. "You said Mr. Neusberg covered for you on the Arsenio Hall show. Would you care to elaborate on that?"

Bobby looked at me then sighed. "Well, I guess I whitewashed it somewhat." He wiped his mouth again and took a sip of coffee from an immaculate china cup. Which he set down in a matching saucer. Cups and saucers that match. What a concept. "Actually, I was fairly upset when it happened and it was stupid not to tell you the truth. I mean, well . . ." Bobby sighed again. "We have . . . had the same agent, Cab and I. Abel Axelrod. Abel's been very good to me, and I don't mean to slight him in the least, but. . . ." He crumpled the linen napkin in his fist. His pale, white-bread face turned a blotchy red. "I'd worked really hard meeting the right people. Getting to the right people. I set the Arsenio gig up myself. But you don't do shit in this business without an agent." Bobby stopped and looked at me.

I looked at Pucci. "That's the truth. Nobody talks to you. They talk to your agent."

Bobby nodded. "But I'd done all the legwork myself, got the right people to see my gig while I was in L.A. Got invited to parties that would do me some good. I spent a year setting it up." Again, he sighed. "A week before I was supposed to appear on Arsenio, Cab called Abel and told him he had some new material he wanted to try out on a TV audience. Abel told him about my gig. Cab said he'd take it." The red color no longer blotched Bobby's face, but covered it like a bad sunburn. "Just like that. And Abel did it. Called me and said, 'Sorry, kid. I need that slot for something else.' My slot. The slot I'd earned."

"Guess you must have been pretty mad at Cab?" Pucci said.

Bobby turned his head quickly to Pucci. "Yeah, you bet your ass I was mad. But I didn't kill him."

Pucci nodded his head and stood up. "Well, thanks for your time, Mr. Rivers." He nodded toward me.

I spread my arms out. "My food's not here!"

"We'll eat later."

I stood up, patted Bobby on the shoulder, and moved off with Detective Pucci.

Once back in the unmarked police car, I said, "I'm really hungry."

"Is that all you think about?"

"No. I only think about food four or five times a day. The rest of the time I think about my routine."

"Yeah? Always thinking, huh?"

"Always."

He pulled out of the covered driveway of the hotel and out into traffic. "What did you think of his story?"

"Well, it gives him a hell of a better motive than I've got."

"What's your motive?" Pucci asked, glancing at me.

I shrugged. "That's just it. I haven't got one."

"What about the fact that you two had a fling in Denver three years ago and, to my informant's knowledge, the other night was the first time you'd heard from him since?"

I folded my arms across my chest. "If I killed every guy who said he'd call me and then didn't, Detective, there'd be dead bodies strung from San Diego to Portland, Maine."

Pucci laughed. "Get around, do you?"

Great. Now he thought I'd slept with guys all over the country. "I said guys who said they'd call, not . . . whatever."

"You're blushing, Ms. Kruse."

"I am not. I have high blood pressure caused by not eating on time."

Pucci pulled the unmarked police car into the parking lot of a Denny's. "This okay?" he asked.

"Fine," I said, sliding out my side of the car and heading for the door.

Behind me, I heard Pucci say, "Save me at least a piece of toast, okay?"

Forty-five minutes later I set down my empty coffee cup for the third time, leaned back on the plastic seat cushion, and sighed.

"Sated?" Pucci asked, raising the eyebrow.

It was definitely a sexual overture. I knew one when I heard one. But being a professional comic, I knew how to give withering comebacks, the likes of which could kill better men than Pucci.

"Yeah," I said.

"What do you know about Joey Scarlotti?" Pucci asked.

I shrugged. "I never met him before the other night. Seen him on Letterman, but never worked with him. Has a decent routine if you're into the I - hate - everybody - and - I'll - tell - you - all - about - it crap. Gets some laughs."

"Any connection with Neusberg?"

I shook my head. "I have no idea." I leaned forward and grinned. "Why don't we go ask him?"

That damn eyebrow went up. "I got me a partner, huh? When'd you get through the academy?"

I leaned back again on the plastic and played with my coffee cup. "Well, I just thought . . . since I came with you to see Bobby . . ."

"I only did that because you were the source of the information I had on Bobby to begin with. Usually, it's not kosher to take a suspect along to interview other suspects."

"You know, I'm gettin' real tired of hearing you call me a suspect."

"You *are* a suspect."

"I know I'm a suspect!" I said too loudly, then looked around at the people staring at me. I looked quickly back to my empty coffee cup. "I know I'm a suspect," I whispered. "You know I'm a suspect. So why do you have to keep saying it?"

Pucci grinned. "Because some of the people at Denny's didn't know you were. Till now."

I stood up and headed for the door. Over my shoulder I said, "I assume breakfast's on you. I'll find my own way back to the hotel."

6

just didn't say which hotel. Babe Marsh and Joey Scarlotti were staying at the same hotel where I'd almost had breakfast that morning with Bobby Rivers. The taxi driver found that hotel easier than he could have found the Lake House. So it seemed the humane thing to do. I knew Pucci would be concentrating on Joey Scarlotti. Therefore, I'd concentrate on Babe Marsh. Besides, Babe liked me. She might accept my visit at her hotel as one of pure friendship. And the questions as just honest curiosity.

The Carlton isn't the type of hotel where they tell you what room a guest is in. The man at the desk said, "If you'll give me your name, I'll call Ms. Marsh's room for you." Then he smiled. A professional smile. One that didn't touch his eyes or cause wrinkles.

I gave him my name, he smiled again, and then dialed the room for Babe Marsh. Luckily, Babe was in. We had one last show to do tonight, then I guess we'd all just hang around until Pucci decided we could leave. Of course, one of us might not ever be leaving. Except to go to whatever the Illinois equivalent of Huntsville is. Oh, yeah, Joliet. Like in the *Blues Brothers*. Maybe, I thought, I should check it out. Just in case. See how big the rooms are and if you can bring your own accessories.

The desk man hung up the phone and turned to me with a smile. "Ms. Marsh says to send you right up. Room fourteen-twenty-three.

1423. Great. The thirteenth floor. Poor Babe. Hotels and other high-rises usually don't allow as they have a thirteenth floor, which means they just skip the number. The fourteenth floor is really the thirteenth floor, so whom are they trying to kid? You can't make something go away just by not calling it by name. Luckily, I'm not superstitious. Much. I mean, I spit on my hand when I see a bale of hay in a moving vehicle, but, then, who doesn't?

Babe greeted me at the door. She was standing there with the door open, blocking the light into the hallway.

"Kimmey!" She hugged me as if we hadn't seen each other since the day before which, when you think about it, we hadn't.

"Hi," I greeted her, "I was in the neighborhood . . ."

Babe ushered me into her room. Two double beds, a desk, a love seat, floor-to-ceiling windows, real carpet on the floor (as opposed to the indoor/outdoor variety at the Lake House), a bathroom with linens (as opposed to a frayed towel and a Handi Wipe for a washcloth), and all the amenities necessary in a first-class establishment.

Babe waved me to the love seat and plopped down on one of the double beds. "Do you think that detective will let us go tomorrow?"

I shrugged. "I have no idea."

"I'm so glad you came to see me," Babe said, smiling widely and patting my knee where I sat on the love seat. Yes, I felt guilty.

"Well," I said, "I thought this would be a good opportunity for us to finally get to know each other better. I mean, we've worked together before, but it just seems there's never time to really talk when you're working."

"Isn't that the truth?" She grinned again and again patted my leg. "This is just great! I've always wanted to talk to you. You know, really get to know you."

I smiled. "Me, too."

"So, tell me," Babe said, "you're from Texas?"

I nodded. "Right. Austin. The capital."

"That must be exciting."

"It's a nice town. Where are you from? Somewhere in Ohio, right?"

"Right. Cincinnati."

"You have brothers and sisters?" I asked.

"Three older sisters by my mother's first husband. They're built like him, Daddy Jack. I've always been big. My daddy was a big man. I never met him, though. He was my mother's second husband. Well, not exactly her husband, but close enough. They had me."

"So you were raised by your mother and her other husband?"

"Oh, no, they were divorced before my mother even met my dad. But I knew Daddy Jack fairly well. He used to come to the house to pick up my sisters for their weekend visitations and stuff. And he'd always say hello to me. He'd ruffle my hair, give me a piece of candy, and say, 'Hi, baby, how you doing?'"

Babe looked at me and smiled. I wanted to cry, but I smiled back. "That's nice," I said, and felt like an idiot.

"I'd watch and wave out the window as my sisters and their daddy drove off in his great big Ford. He got a new one every year. I always wanted to go for a drive in one of his new Fords, but it never worked out. My father's name was John McCormick. But I have the same last name as my mom and my sisters. Since they never got married, my parents I mean."

I nodded my head in agreement. "I would think that probably worked out for the best."

She went on as if I hadn't spoken. "He died, Mom said, right before I was born. She didn't know his parents and since he never told them about me, I never got around to meeting them or anything. It was very tragic. The way he died, I mean. He went out for a pack of cigarettes. Luckies, I think. There was this holdup at the liquor store on the corner. Some Puerto Rican, Mom said, shot my daddy. I was born a few months later. Like I said, it was all very tragic."

"Yes," I said, nodding.

"But I had a good childhood," Babe said, smiling up at me, remembering I was in the room. "Mom was a nurse. An LVN. She did a lot of home-duty stuff. She'd stay at sick people's houses and take care of them. Usually the night shift. And every night when she left, she'd look at my sisters and say, 'Take care of the baby!' " Babe laughed and I imitated her.

"That's how I got my name. Babe. It just got shortened from 'baby.' My real name's Marilyn. Marilyn Marsh. But nobody calls me that. Not even my mother. I think my father would have, though."

"That's a pretty name," I said.

"Isn't it, though? Anyway, my sisters were good to me. They loved me a lot. They used to dress me up like I was a doll. We always had a lot of fun together. Sometimes, though, when I got older, around six or seven, they'd go off and leave me alone. But I never told on them. Not once. They were real pretty, my big sisters. And boys came by a lot and they'd go out. And they were so much older than me and all. The sister closest to me, Brenda, was eight when I was born. They were small. Not like you," she said, smiling, "taller, but skinny. Sometimes, if they didn't go out, especially Brenda, she'd bring her boyfriends in. They'd spend most of the time in the bedroom she and I shared. I'd just stay in the living room and watch TV. My sisters would always leave me things when they went out, like bags of potato chips and sodas and candy bars, and, sometimes, when Brenda or Candace or Olivia had boys over, the boys would bring me pizzas of my very own. And ice cream. It wasn't a bad child-hood at all."

"It sounds very loving," I said.

"It was. We were great friends. But then they started moving out. The last one, Brenda, moved out when I was ten. Got her an apartment with a boy. They never came home much after that. It was just Mama and me. But we took good care of each other."

I wanted to cry. I wanted to hold her and call her Marilyn and cry. I couldn't help wondering when the last time had been that someone had said to Babe Marsh, "Let's talk." I didn't know how to stop the flow and get to my real mission, which made me feel ashamed, guilty, and just a tinge angry at Babe for being so damned needy.

"Enough about me," Babe said, as if she'd been reading my mind, "Bobby said you were with that detective this morning. He didn't say anything about how long he might keep us?"

"No, I didn't have the nerve to find out. He just wanted to ask Bobby some questions and I got to come along for the ride."

"About the Arsenio fiasco," Babe said.

I nodded.

"Poor Bobby. It seems like such an unlikely thing for Cab to do. He was such a nice man."

My opening. "Did you know him before this gig?"

Babe nodded, her multiple chins flapping in the breeze. "I worked with him about six months ago in Atlanta. Very gentlemanly."

"What do you know about Joey Scarlotti?"

Babe cocked her head at me in a quizzical fashion. "In what way?"

"In connection with Cab."

Babe looked down at her ample body. "I'm sure I wouldn't know."

There was one thing I definitely knew about Babe Marsh as of that moment. She was an awful liar.

"Babe?"

She looked up, her eyes darting from me to the window behind me, to the desk, to anywhere but my eyes. "Yes?"

Babe Marsh was a very sympathetic type. I decided to go for the pity ploy. "Babe, I'm afraid I'm everybody's favorite suspect. If there was something between Joey and Cab, I really need to know."

She sighed and folded her arms across her chest, or I should say, attempted to. I know, I'm a bitch. "I really don't know any details. . . ."

"That's okay," I encouraged, "I'll take rumor and innuendo. I ain't proud."

Babe laughed. "You're so funny!" Sobering, she said, "There was something about a girl in Omaha. You know, Joey's a very sweet person, but he's not exactly the type girls go crazy for."

I nodded. I agreed Joey Scarlotti wasn't exactly the type girls go for. He was about five feet four inches tall, weighed barely more than I did, had a weasel face, rotten teeth, and thin hair he plastered to his scalp in an attempt to hide bald spots. I didn't agree that he was a very sweet person. As far as I knew, Joey Scarlotti was an asshole. But then, I'm prejudiced against people who tend to think my pain and torment is solely for their amusement. I'm funny that way. "What happened?" I asked.

Babe shook her head. "I'm not sure. Like I said,

I don't have all the details. I wasn't there. This is all just hearsay." She sighed. "Kimmey, I really hate to be a rumormonger."

That's okay, I thought, mong, mong! I sighed. "Babe, I could go to prison for something I didn't do."

"Oh, dear." She sighed again, a sigh so deep her entire body moved with it. "As I understand it, Joey brought his girlfriend with him from New York to the gig in Omaha. Like I said, I don't know the details, but she left after only a couple of nights." She looked down at the bed. "Somebody said that somebody else saw her leaving Cab's room that night. And then she and Joey had a knock down, drag out fight." She shrugged. "That's just what I heard and I'm not sure any of it's really true."

I thanked her and got up to leave.

Babe stood up. "Oh, do you have to leave so soon?"

"I'm afraid so. But I'm so glad we got this chance to talk."

Babe smiled. "Oh, it was my pleasure. I hardly ever get company."

I left feeling sufficiently guilty. Running into Pucci in the lobby just made it worse.

"Ms. Kruse."

"Detective Mucci."

He folded his arms across his chest. "I have an idea. Why don't you just call me by my first name?"

"Okay, Cal," I said.

"Sal!" He shook his head then looked at me. "Don't do that anymore."

I shrugged my shoulders and raised my hands, the picture of total innocence. "Do what?"

He raised the eyebrow. "What brings you back to the Carlton?"

"Did you interview Scarlotti?" Answer a question with a question whenever you don't want to answer. I learned that from watching politicians.

"Yes." The closemouthed bastard.

"Well?"

"Well, what?"

I sighed. Pucci was fast becoming one of my least favorite people. Right up there with the current administration and my tenth-grade English teacher. "What did he have to say?" I asked.

"I'm sorry, Ms. Kruse. That's strictly confidential."

"Did he mention Cab sleeping with Joey's girlfriend in Omaha? And Joey and his girlfriend breaking up over it?"

The eyebrow business. "Where'd you hear this?"

I grinned. "I have my sources."

He didn't grin back. "Which are?"

I kept on grinning. "I'm sorry, Sal, that's strictly confidential."

"If all I have is your word for it, Ms. Kruse, I'm afraid I'll have to chalk that up to the number one suspect just trying to shove the blame onto somebody else."

The man certainly knew how to tick me off. "How can I possibly be anybody's number one suspect? I'm one of the few people in the world who liked the guy!"

"And I only have your word for that."

I sighed. "Babe Marsh told me."

The eyebrow. I figured with all the exercise he gave that little muscle he could probably pick up a dump truck with the hair. "Have you been interviewing suspects, Ms. Kruse?"

"What? I can't come see a friend and colleague?"

Pucci moved into my space, his pointed finger only millimeters from my pert little nose. "Stay out of this, Ms. Kruse. You have no business getting involved. Just go back to your hotel and stay there until you have to be at the comedy club."

"Is that an order?"

He backed off a hair. "Of course not. I have no right to order you to do anything. . . ."

"Damned straight!"

"But . . ." He grinned. An evil, malevolent grin. "I'm suggesting ever so politely that you bug off, Ms. Kruse. Stay out of my way."

"I have a question," I said.

"No doubt," he replied.

"Why did you insist on bringing me with you to interview Bobby this morning?"

"Because the information I had came from your source." He grinned again. "And because I thought it might be interesting to see what you look like in the morning."

"Don't flirt with me, Pucci. It gets on my nerves."

"Is that an order?"

I grinned. "I'm just suggesting ever so politely that you bug off."

I turned and headed for the Carlton's revolving door.

* * *

I took a taxi to the Kaiser Komedy Klub. It's okay, it's tax deductible. I still knew nothing about several players in our little scenario. Like Bucky Schwartz, Mickey Reynolds, and the no-name lady agent. I figured Bert could fill me in a little. I also figured it wouldn't hurt if I overheard another telephone conversation.

I found him in his office, talking on the phone. He waved me to the couch and kept on talking. Unfortunately, I knew exactly what this phone call was about.

"Baby, baby, listen! I want you! With all my heart and soul! But it's these Chicago audiences. They don't know funny. I swear to you. They thought Belushi was funny. What can I say? Look, I got somebody in my office. I'll call you, babe, I swear. Love ya."

He put down the phone and looked at me. "Kimmey . . ."

I could feel the mad look on my face. "Belushi *was* funny!" I said.

"Of course he was funny," Bert said, then pointed with his thumb toward the phone. "But that numb-nuts isn't." He grinned. "What can I do for my favorite redhead?"

"What's that woman's name who was with Cab the other night? The manager type?"

He leaned back in his swivel chair. "Rea Carmody. She's a pistol, huh?"

"I wouldn't know, I never saw her off the phone."

"A real go-getter, that gal. Handles about six comics. Not many, yeah, but all her guys are hot.

Really hot. Just took on Cab a couple of months ago. If Rea takes you on, you know you're on your way up. You want an intro?"

"No, I'm doing fine with Myra right now."

"Rea's not an agent. She's a personal manager. Handles PR and investments, that kinda stuff. I'm telling you, honey-buns, you should try her. After all, she's got an opening."

I shook my head. "I don't think I'm big enough for somebody like that." I leaned forward. "Anyway, I just wanted to know her name. Is she staying at the Carlton?"

"Naw, Rea lives here in Chicago. Got a condo off Lakeshore in the north." He riffled his Rolodex. "You want the address?"

I nodded my head and took the card, writing down the address on a piece of scrap paper from my purse. "What about Bucky Schwartz?"

"Staying in Cab's bus." He pointed his thumb toward his window. "Out there in the back parking lot."

"And Mickey Reynolds?"

Bert leaned forward. "What's going on, Kimmey? What are you doing?"

What could I tell Bert Kaiser? After what I'd heard him say on the phone, telling somebody "everything'd been taken care of"? Maybe the "everything" he referred to was Cab Neusberg. How was I to know? But if I didn't tell him what I was doing, would he give me Mickey Reynolds's address? Once again those nasty horns of a dilemma were tickling my butt.

I sighed. "Bert, do you think I killed Cab?"

Bert's face fused into a look of total concern as

he leaned across and grasped my arm in his hairy hand. "Of course not! Baby, who would?"

"The police. And the DA's office. And probably my mother. But, Bert, I didn't do it."

He patted my hand. "I know that, sweetheart. Believe me, I know that!"

"But somebody did. While the police are looking at me, I need to be finding out who had a motive. That's why I want the addresses of Bucky Schwartz, Rea Carmody, and Mickey Reynolds."

Bert leaned back and again riffled his Rolodex, handing me a card with Mickey Reynolds's address on it. It wasn't nearly as uptown as Rea Carmody's.

As I got up to leave, Bert stood and moved around his desk, seizing me in a bear hug. "You do what you gotta do, doll, and know I'm one hundred percent behind you!"

When I could breathe again, I thanked him and left, heading out the back way for Cab's bus and an interview with Bucky Schwartz.

I knocked on the door of the bus. It was one of those specialty numbers, with a paint job to rival any country crooner's. Clown faces and the comedy mask adorned it. But nobody answered the door. I walked around it, called Bucky's name a few times, then headed for the front of the club, where there was a bus stop. My handy Chicago Transit Authority map showed me that I could get to Rea Carmody's condo in three transfers. Mickey Reynolds's was a straight shot through Old Town, then a short two-block walk. I decided to try Mickey first.

The building was a crumbling tenement in a

row of crumbling tenements. Three blocks east was the avant garde district. Three blocks west rose refurbished, upwardly mobile dwellings. Mickey Reynolds had managed to find himself his own little pocket of poverty.

The foyer smelled like pee and I heard the pitter-patter of little feet behind the walls and, somehow, I got the impression the rats they belonged to weren't of the rug variety. Mickey was on the third floor. As there was no elevator, I hit the stairs. Mickey's door was adorned with a card taped to it with his name and a happy face with a line through it. I knocked and the door swung open in front of me.

Okay, I've watched enough TV in lonely hotel rooms to know what that means. But that's TV, not reality, right? I pushed the door open wider and called out Mickey's name. There was no answer. I must admit I wasn't totally surprised when I went in and saw Mickey's body sprawled across the kitchenette floor—repulsed, sickened, terrified, but not totally surprised.

7

I sat on the top step of the stoop waiting for Pucci, my elbows on my knees, my chin cupped in my hands. I was planning what I'd wear on the first day of my trial. Something demure and innocent. Long-skirted and high-necked.

Pucci's unmarked squad car pulled up with his little cherry-top light blazing, followed close behind by a patrol car. I stood up. I felt like a kid who'd just gotten caught playing doctor in the bedroom with the boy next door. And here came Daddy. Pucci parked illegally, opened the door, and got out, slamming it loudly behind him. He walked up to me.

"Where is it?"

I pointed behind me. "Third floor. Room three-twenty-four."

He grabbed my upper arm and escorted me back into the building. Once at Mickey Reynolds's door, I balked.

"I think I'll stay out here, if you don't mind. I've already had the pleasure of his company."

"In," he said. I went in. "Is everything exactly as you found it?"

"Except for my fingerprints on the doorknob and the telephone receiver."

"Shit. Why don't you ever wear gloves?"

"Because I'm innocent, that's why!"

He glared at me and pulled on rubber gloves from his back pocket.

"You got any more of those?" I asked.

He glared again and began studying the room, moving slowly to Mickey's body lying on the floor of the kitchenette. Once there, he squatted and began examining the body. I excused myself and headed for the front door, only to be stopped by a uniformed officer.

"Detective Pucci wants for you to stay put," the man informed me.

I went to the grimy window overlooking the grimy street and stared off into space. It beat the hell out of staring at Mickey Reynolds's body. There was no blood. I was thankful for that. Like Cab before him, Mickey was just dead.

"Neck looks broken," Pucci said.

I turned. "Well, that sure as hell clears me. Do I look like I could break somebody's neck?"

"We'll wait for the ME to make it official. Maybe he can figure out a way a pipsqueak like you coulda done it," Pucci said.

I turned back to the window. Mickey Reynolds

had been about five foot eleven. A little on the heavy side. I'm five foot one and weigh ninety-eight pounds after a heavy meal. Even Pucci could see it would be impossible. But we waited.

"You don't have to come in with me," I said, as Pucci parked the car illegally in front of the Lake House.

"My pleasure," he said, getting out and following me in.

"I haven't had any dinner and I plan on eating," I told him.

He smiled. It was a cold smile. "Great. I'll join you."

"I don't remember asking."

"Be nice, Kruse. Be thankful you're not in lockup."

"For what?" I demanded, stopping, hands on hips. "I didn't do anything! You know that!"

"I don't know squat about what you did or didn't do, Kruse. All I know is you have a real bad habit of being in the wrong place at the wrong time."

"The ME told you Mickey'd been dead for over twelve hours! He also told you it would have been next to impossible for little ol' me to break the neck of somebody that much bigger than I am."

"The ME doesn't know you."

We stood nose to nose in the lobby of the Lake House. He was wearing Old Spice again. Or Aqua Velva. I was going to have to ask. His five-o'clock shadow looked denser than some guys' three-month growth. And I couldn't help noticing his eyes weren't really black. More a dark brown with flecks of gold. And he had a mole. . . .

I turned and walked into the dining room and found a table. I *wasn't* attracted to this man. I like men at least twice my height. Pucci was short. I like men with blue eyes. Pucci's eyes were very dark. I like men with baby-smooth faces, not gorillas. So then why was I behaving like a heroine in a bad romance novel? Excuse me, that's redundant.

Pucci followed me into the dining room and picked up a menu left on the table. "So," he said, "what's for dinner?"

I grabbed the menu out of his hands and scanned the typewritten daily special. Meatloaf, mashed potatoes and cream gravy, corn, salad, and a dinner roll. It would suffice. My metabolism being what it is, I'd probably have to raid the candy machine later, but the special could get me by.

Max came up to the table. "Today's special and a six-pack," I told him.

He looked at Pucci. "Same. And I'll share her six-pack."

Max turned tail and ran, the coward.

"I don't remember asking you to share," I said.

"Got a joke for you. . . ."

"Pa—leeze!"

"Lighten up, Kruse. Anyway, the Lone Ranger gets captured by some renegade Indians—"

"I'm not in the mood for this."

"And they start to tie him to the stake . . ."

"Hello? Can anyone hear me?"

". . . but he tells them that it's traditional among his people that the condemned man get one last wish."

"What about condemned women? What do we get? Besides bad jokes from fascist cops?"

"The Indians agree, so the Lone Ranger whispers in Trigger's ear—"

"Trigger was Roy Rogers's horse. The Lone Ranger's horse was Silver."

"Good, you're listening. But I don't think it matters what color the horse is. . . ."

"That's his name, stupid!"

"Oh. So he whispers in Silver's ear and Silver gallops off. Pretty soon he comes back with a gorgeous naked blond strapped to his saddle . . ."

"Why did I know naked women would somehow come up?"

". . . and the Indians start laughing and clapping and start to set up a tepee, but the Lone Ranger says, 'No!' and whispers in Trigger's—"

"Silver!"

"—Silver's ear again and Silver gallops off and comes back with a gorgeous naked brunette. . . ."

"Spare me."

Max brought our food and sat down, his face all grins, ready to hear the rest of the stupid joke.

"And the Lone Ranger says, 'No!' and whispers in Silver's ear again and the horse gallops off and comes back with a . . ."

"A gorgeous naked buffalo?"

". . . a gorgeous naked redhead," Pucci said, glaring at me, then to Max he said, "Finally, the Lone Ranger walks up to Silver and says, 'Silver, read my lips! I said posse!'"

Max laughed like an idiot while I devoured my meatloaf. Amateurs. Tracy came up and leaned against Max. He put his arm around her waist and I sighed inwardly while the theme music to the "Love Boat" rattled around my brain.

"You know how many blonds it takes to make chocolate-chip cookies?" Max asked Pucci.

Tracy nudged him with her hip. "Not fair!"

"No, how many?" Pucci asked.

"Two. One to mix the batter and one to peel the M&M's."

"You know how to totally frustrate a blond?" Pucci asked.

Max giggled but shook his head.

"Give her a bag of M&M's and tell her to alphabetize them."

Max leaned forward. "Did you hear about the blond who lost her job at the M&M factory because she threw out all the Ws?"

I could see they were on a roll, so I finished the last of the food on my plate, grabbed the four beers left in the six-pack, and headed for the door. Pucci wasn't far behind me.

"Good night," I said in the lobby, heading purposefully for the elevator.

Pucci followed. At the elevator door, I said, "Good night!"

"I'll walk you to your room," he said.

"You don't have to do that."

"Yes, I do," he said. "I was raised by an Italian mother."

We got silently into the elevator and rode up to the fourth floor. When we got to my room, he said, "Besides, there's always the off chance you may have changed your mind."

"About what?" I asked, juggling the beer to get to my key.

"Sleeping with me."

I opened the door and deposited the beer and my purse on the chair inside the door, just in case I needed my hands free to defend myself.

"I wouldn't sleep with you if you were the last man on earth," I said.

Pucci grinned. "The way guys are dropping dead around you, Kruse, we may be putting that to the test real soon." He turned and left.

I went into my room, popped the top on a semi-cold one, and dialed Phoebe's ten digits.

"Hello?" she said.

"Mickey Reynolds got killed tonight."

"Who's Mickey Reynolds?"

"The emcee at the club."

"Is it related to Cab?"

"Pucci thinks so."

"What does Pucci know?" Phoebe reminded me.

"Not much," I admitted. "But, then again, it certainly looks related."

"Digitalis?"

"No. Broken neck."

"So maybe he fell?"

"Dream on." I sighed.

"What's the problem?" Phoebe asked.

"Besides finding a dead body and having Pucci hot for *my* bod? Both punitively and sexually."

"You found this guy?"

"Yes," I admitted, somewhat hesitantly.

"Were you alone?"

"Yes."

"Kimberly Anne Kruse. Just stop it! No more dead bodies!"

"Yes, Mother," I said.

Phoebe sighed. "Have you called Hazlet?"

"They didn't even take me downtown. The ME more or less cleared me. Mickey'd been dead twelve hours when I found the body and he was also a lot bigger than me."

"So? There's any number of ways you could have done it."

I took the phone away from my ear and tapped the receiver with my fingernail. "Hello? Hello?" I said. "I thought I was talking to someone who was on my side."

"I am on your side."

"Then come up here and help me!" I demanded.

"I can't. I'm due in court tomorrow morning at nine on a case that could drag on a year or more. And we have a judge who doesn't believe in substituting counsel."

"Oh, sure, come up with excuses."

"Call Hazlet."

"He doesn't know me," I whined. "He probably thinks I did it."

"That's okay," Phoebe said. "Most of his clients are probably guilty. But he gets them off."

"Yeah, right, and the innocent ones go to jail."

"You're whining."

"I have a right."

"They haven't charged you with anything," Phoebe reminded me.

"Not yet."

"Has Pucci made another pass?"

"Yes. Tonight," I said.

"Have you told Hazlet?"

I sighed. "Well, no. I haven't talked to Hazlet since we took that bottle of digitalis in."

"I told you to tell him about Pucci coming on to you!"

"I know. . . ."

"So," Phoebe was getting her queen-of-the-universe voice on, "why didn't you?"

"I don't want to get him in trouble. . . ."

"The problem with sexual harassment is that it's only harassment if the woman doesn't want the man coming on to her."

"I don't want him coming—"

"Bull crackers," she said.

"I told him to drop dead!" I paraphrased.

"Not a good thing to be telling people right now, Kimmey."

"Well, those weren't my exact words."

I could hear Phoebe rummaging through her kitchen while we talked. "What are you eating?" I asked.

"Nothing."

"Phoebe."

"Celery."

"Phoebe."

She sighed. "With cream cheese. It's very good." I could hear her crunch the celery. "Okay. Down to business. Why would whoever killed Cab want to kill this Mickey person?"

"Hell, I don't know why they killed Cab, so how can I know why they killed Mickey?"

"You used to be an investigator. Think."

"I wasn't that kind of investigator. I read medical records, for God's sake."

"And interviewed witnesses and found out the truth . . ."

"And did my best to cover up the truth half the time for mother insurance company," I reminded her.

"That's beside the point. That's just legal games. We all do that."

"Noble profession you belong to, Phoeb."

"Think!" she ordered.

"Okay. Mickey saw the person who put the digitalis in Cab's drink. Or wherever. And was blackmailing him. I read that in an Agatha Christie, I think."

"Or?" Phoebe encouraged.

"Or. He saw and didn't know he saw it and the killer decided to do away with him before something jogged his memory. Nero Wolfe."

"Or?"

"Or. Mickey was the real victim all along and Cab was just a subterfuge. Matt Houston, I think."

"Yeah. I saw that one. Where all these brides were being killed and they thought it was a serial killer. . . ."

"Phoebe."

"That was during their bimbo-kill-list-of-the-week phase. Serial killer after brides, serial killer after beauty queens, serial killer after center-folds . . ."

"Phoebe."

"Right. He was a hunk, though, wasn't he?"

"Phoebe!"

"What?"

"I think I might be in trouble."

"Oh, God, you slept with Pucci and now you're pregnant."

"Not that kind of trouble! And no, I didn't and I won't sleep with Pucci! Jeeze! I think they're going to arrest me."

"Then call Hazlet!"

"First thing in the morning," I said.

"Promise?"

"Promise. I gotta go. Tonight's the last set at the club."

"Stay in the presence of other people—preferably two or more—at all times," Phoebe warned.

"Yes, Mother."

I hung up and got dressed for the club.

8

I dressed in white ribbed tights, black ankle boots, black suede hiking shorts, a white cotton sweater, and a black and white junior-high letter jacket I picked up at a garage sale in Green Bay, Wisconsin. It had red letters on it for color. I looked in the mirror. I looked cute. Of course, I always looked cute. Never gorgeous. Never beautiful. Never even extremely sexy. Just cute. Personally, I hate cute.

I always wear black and white on stage. I once read an interview with Lucille Ball where she said she always wore those colors because they stand out on TV. I haven't made it to TV yet, but I consider this practice. And yes, Phoebe was right, I do have a Lucille Ball complex.

I took a taxi to the club and went straight to the

green room. It was twenty minutes to show time and all suspects were accounted for; well, almost all. Rea Carmody and Bucky Schwartz were missing. I'd have to interview those two sometime.

Bobby Rivers was sitting in a corner by himself, studying a Sharper Image catalog; Joey Scarlotti was pacing; and Babe Marsh was taking up the love seat, her eyes on the floor, avoiding contact with everyone.

When I walked in the room, Joey stopped pacing. "You bitch!"

I looked at him. *"Moi?"*

"Who the fuck died and left you queen of the fucking world?"

"Joey, you're repeating your obscenities. Decidedly uncool," I said, heading for the couch and lying down. I deal with animosity much better while in a prone position.

"You sicced that goddamn dago cop on me!" Joey said—or screamed. Whatever.

"Such ethnic slurs," I said. "Tsk, tsk. And against one of your own."

I felt his shadow pass over my closed eyes. I opened one. Yep. He was standing over me, spittle showing at the sides of his mouth.

"Get up, bitch! I'm talking to you!" He slapped me on the arm. I jumped up, but Babe Marsh already had him cornered against the wall, her finger poking his nose.

"You don't hit ladies, Joey!" she said, her voice almost raised. "Didn't your mother teach you that?"

"That bitch ain't no lady!"

"Now, Joey! Stop that swearing!" Babe said.

I touched her arm. "It's okay, Babe. Let him get it out of his system."

Babe backed off and Joey moved around her to glare at me. "If you weren't a broad I'd bust you in the chops!"

I laughed. "Come on, Joey, the only kind of person you could bust in the chops would be a broad!"

He drew back, I ducked, and Detective Pucci walked into the room.

"What's going on here?" he demanded.

Joey sat down in the easy chair, Babe grabbed her love seat, and I plopped down on the couch and closed my eyes. It was going to be difficult being funny tonight.

"Nothing," Joey answered, "just somebody came in here that doesn't belong, that's all."

I sat up. "Tell me, Joey, did you confess to the detective what really happened when Cab screwed your girlfriend?"

Joey spread his arms wide. "Hey, no big deal. I mean, Cab'd fuck anything. After all, he fucked you."

"You jerk."

"Slut."

"Mother—"

I stopped in midword due to the applause. I swung my head around to see Pucci holding up the wall and slowly clapping his hands. "What's with you?" I demanded.

He shoved his hands in his pockets. "You two. You need to take this on the road. Make a great act."

I lay back down on the couch, crossed my arms

over my breasts, and closed my eyes. I was just going to pretend they weren't there.

But Pucci was having none of that. "Ms. Kruse," he said, disturbing my much needed rest, "I'd like to see you in Bert Kaiser's office."

I heard the door slam, presumably behind him, and got up from my position on the couch to follow. As I got to the door, Joey Scarlotti said, "Bitch."

I turned and smiled at Joey. "No wonder your girlfriend would rather go to bed with Cab than you."

I skedaddled out of the room as he bounded out of his chair. He didn't follow me out into the hall. I assumed Babe had him cornered again. I'd have to thank her. I doubted Joey Scarlotti had any compunction about coldcocking women.

When I got to Bert Kaiser's office, I found Pucci sitting in Bert's office chair, his feet resting on the papers on top of Bert's desk.

"My, don't we look comfortable," I said, slouching down in the chair opposite the desk.

Pucci looked at me. He didn't raise an eyebrow. He didn't sneer. He didn't grin. It was the least animated I'd ever seen him. "What was that shit with you and Scarlotti?"

I shrugged. "He didn't like the fact that I told you about his girlfriend and Cab. He got offensive."

"You, on the other hand, remained your demure little self."

"Hey," I said, "just verbal self-defense."

He pulled his little notebook out of his inside coat pocket while I thought hard to remember any other transgressions of my past. But I could think of nary a one.

"You ever heard of Don Resson?" he asked me.

"Don Resson . . . yeah. He's a comic. I don't know him, though."

"Ever work with him?"

"No," I said, emphasizing the word. "I said I didn't know him. If I'd worked with him, I'd know him, now wouldn't I?"

"What about Mike Burley?"

I shook my head. "Never heard of him."

"He's a comic."

I shook my head again. "I still have never heard of him. Why? Who are these two guys?"

"The better question would be: Who *were* these two guys. Don Resson was killed two months ago by a hit-and-run driver while he was jogging outside his home in Portland, Oregon. Mike Burley died of cardiac arrest due to an overdose of digitalis three weeks ago. Dropped dead during a performance at a comedy club in Battle Creek, Michigan. Surprised you didn't read it in the papers or hear about it on TV."

I shook my head. "Three weeks ago I was on a cruise ship off the Florida coast. No papers. No TV. Except dirty movies piped in." I pulled myself up into a fetal sitting position, arms around my knees, knees drawn to my chest. "I take it this has something to do with Cab."

"It would seem so. We're checking it out now."

"Had either of them worked with Cab?"

"Like I said, we're checking it out now. Mike Burley's wife said she thought he had. She'd heard of Cab Neusberg, but she couldn't remember when.

She said Mike was on the road a lot and she was divorcing him, so she hadn't paid a lot of attention." He flipped his little notebook to another page. "We've got both their agents' names and, first thing in the morning, we'll call and find out their schedules for the last year. See if we can find anything that matches up."

I took a deep breath. "Why are you telling me this? Instead of telling everybody?"

"Because you're the only one of that bunch I'm sure didn't do it."

I almost peed in my pants. "Why?" I asked, my voice barely above a whisper.

"Because, according to your agent, Myra Mitchell, when Mike Burley was killed you were on a cruise ship off the Florida coast. . . ."

"I just told you that."

He grinned. ". . . and when Don Resson was killed, you were on a puddle jumper going from Boston to Concord, New Hampshire. Your name's on the manifest and the one steward remembers you because you're so damned cute."

I was grateful Pucci didn't take that minute to ask me to sleep with him. I woulda jumped on his bones in a New York minute. "Thank God that part of this nightmare's over," I said.

"You wanna sleep with me now?" Pucci asked.

I stood up and walked to the door. "You're an asshole, Pucci."

He grinned. "Yeah, but at least you remember my name."

"I was wonderful," I told Phoebe.

"You always are," she said.

I held the phone away from my ear and looked at it. Maybe I'd dialed the wrong number. "I'm sorry," I said, "I wanted to speak to Phoebe R. *Love.*"

"Don't be a bitch, Kim."

"What's wrong, Phoeb?"

"Nothing."

"Of course something's wrong. You're only nice to me when you're in a severe depression."

"That's not true, I'm always ni—Nathaniel called."

"Oh," I said.

"He wants a divorce."

"Oh," I said.

"He's willing to waive all marital rights."

"Oh?" I said.

"He doesn't want community property or any other kind of settlement and he said he'd sign whatever papers necessary for me to have the house free and clear."

"Oh?" I said.

There was silence on the other end. I didn't know what to say. Nathaniel had been refusing to divorce her for three years unless she paid him off. I knew what this meant.

"Look," I finally said, breaking the silence. "At least he's off your back and onto somebody else's."

"Her name's Annette Swigley," Phoebe said dejectedly.

"Any kin to the Swigley Savings and Loans?"

"The daughter thereof."

"I thought he was in jail. Swigley, I mean."

"No, darlin', you thought he *should* be in jail. There's a difference."

"Well . . ." I said.

"Yeah. But enough. I'm glad things went well for you tonight. I'm glad you're no longer a suspect and I'm glad you're funny again."

"Thank you." I let a beat pass, trying to think of the right thing to say. "So come up here this weekend. The judge can't keep you in Austin on the weekends, too, right?"

"Thanks. I'll think about it. But what I see myself doing this weekend is cleaning out the grease trap under the sink and clearing the gutters."

"He's not worth it, Phoeb."

"He was once. Or so I thought. I gotta go, Kimmey."

I sat cross-legged on my bed at the Lake House listening to a dial tone buzzing on the phone, then I gently laid the receiver in the cradle. Poor Phoebe. The really rotten thing was she had truly loved Nathaniel. And maybe she still did. I sometimes wondered why he had married her. Had he been sincere at the time? Did he think he could be a good husband and a good provider? Did he think he and Phoebe would grow old and gray together? Or did he just think Phoebe would be a solid base for him? Someone to come home to after his womanizing? Someone to support him in and out of his various jobs and schemes? I hated Nathaniel with every fiber of my being. He had hurt my friend. If he were to die from an overdose of digitalis, Pucci could certainly look in my direction.

Pucci. I'd wanted to tell Phoebe about Pucci. I lay down on the bed and looked at the ceiling. Okay. I found Pucci attractive. I had to admit it. At least to myself. I wondered what it would be like to get whisker burn from ten minutes of kissing Pucci. He wasn't my type, certainly, but then, what was my type? Usually, the kind of man I could never really attract. But Pucci was funny and he was smart. He was also a pint-sized hunk. If he'd ask me out to dinner, yeah, I'd probably say yes. But he hadn't asked. All he ever asked was, "You wanna sleep with me?" The sleaze. What kind of insensitive sleaze would ask a woman who'd just had a guy drop dead in the sack with her to go to bed? Couldn't he see that was being unbelievably gauche?

I sat up and began undressing for my shower. Face it, I told myself, Pucci's a creep. A cute creep who could raise one eyebrow and make me laugh, but a creep just the same.

There was a knock at my door at seven o'clock the next morning. I realized when I woke up one of the main reasons I've never bought a gun. Because at that moment I would have started shooting and asked questions later.

I pulled on my robe and stumbled to the door, opening it against the chain. Glaring out I saw Joey Scarlotti standing on the carpet of the hallway of the Lake House. I shut the door, leaned against it, and wondered if I just crawled back into bed would he go away? Deciding he probably wouldn't, being the tenacious little asshole he was, I opened the door, chain securely in place.

"What, Scarlotti?"

"We gotta talk, Kimmey."

The irrational thought struck me that this disgusting little weasel might have decided to find me attractive and, thus, make my life a living hell. But, on the other hand, maybe he was here to finish what he'd started the night before.

"Why?" I asked.

"I didn't kill nobody, you gotta believe me."

Good, I thought. He's just afraid for his life, not after my bod, for any one of multiple reasons. I wasn't really disappointed.

Closing the door to remove the chain, I opened it and moved away to allow him access. I flopped down cross-legged on my unmade bed. Scarlotti stretched out on the love seat, covering his eyes with his arm.

"I been up all night. First that asshole cop of yours kept me at the club till after four grilling me—and everybody else—and then I just been walking around." He removed the arm from his eyes. "I didn't do nothin', Kimmey. You gotta believe that."

"What difference does it matter what I believe, Joey?"

He swung his legs over the side of the love seat and sat up, elbows on knees, and gave me his sincere look. "'Cause if you know the truth, then maybe you can convince that cop of the truth."

I was cleared now. I didn't need to know "the truth" of all the other suspects. But what about Cab? He was still dead. And would be for a long time. Maybe I owed it to him, for some reason, to follow this through. Besides, I didn't have another gig for a week.

"Okay," I said, "so what is 'the truth'?" I asked, making the quote sign with my fingers.

Scarlotti lay back down on the couch and covered his eyes again with his arm. "Okay. That deal in Omaha. Yeah. Cab made it with this chick I had with me that weekend. But it was no big deal. She was just a broad I picked up at my last gig. In Michigan. Her name was Wanda something. I don't even remember what. She had big tits so I let her tag along."

"Scarlotti, you're a real romantic."

He snorted. "Don't tell me nothing about romance, Kruse. I got a story could break your heart. Only been one woman in my life. Now she's married and got three kids. The rest's all just poontang."

"Didn't it make you mad that Cab slept with the lady that was supposed to be with you? I mean, in this day and age, sharing's not what it's cracked up to be."

He took his arm off his eyes and turned his head to look at me. "Yeah, it pissed me off. But not at Cab. I was paying this broad's way, ya know? I paid for her room, her food, her transportation. Bought her a little shit. And she fucking screws somebody else. So I knocked her upside the head and told her to find her own way back to Michigan. On her back, if necessary."

"You are a human being and a gentleman, Scarlotti, you know that?"

"Hey, you're a chick. You got a different style. Me? That's the way I do things. That's just me. I ain't asking you to like it, Kruse. Just accept that I didn't give a rat's ass who Cab Neusberg screwed. I just wasn't gonna pay for it."

"Tell me about the lady with the three kids," I said.

"Get lost, Kruse."

"Was she an older woman you knew once or what?"

He sat up again and looked at me. His eyes were red-rimmed from booze and lack of sleep, the comic's trademark. "We was kids together. A long time ago."

"I can't imagine you as a kid," I said.

Joey snorted. "Yeah, you can. You can see me. The little, skinny Eye-tie sitting in the back row, trying to be invisible. But the WASPs and the niggers and spicks—to them I wasn't fuckin' invisible. To them I was the fuckin' Eye-tie in the back row. So, somewhere, sometime, I learned if they was gonna laugh at me anyway, beat me up and laugh at my ass, I'd beat 'em to the punch, ya know? So I started making 'em laugh. Make a stupid, fuckin' face, tell some dumb ass joke, ya know? So I was in control. *Me*. They stopped beating me up." He looked at me then. "Mind if I lay on the bed?"

"Of course not," I said, getting up. He could lie on my bed, but not with me in it. I moved to the love seat and curled up while Joey Scarlotti stretched out on my bed. "So what happened?" I asked.

Scarlotti shrugged. "They kinda made me their mascot. In high school, I tagged along. Part of the gang, like, ya know? Me and five niggers, a spick, and a WASP. I was the fuckin' comic relief. But that was okay. 'Cause they stopped beating me up."

He sighed. "That's when I met her, though. Virgie Washington. One of the niggers' sisters, Reggie Washington, the big one. Virgie didn't laugh at me. She liked me. And I liked her. But she was a, ya know, nigger. In Brooklyn, back in the midsixties, they didn't go for that. An Eye-tie and a nigger girl. Not even the niggers went for that shit. But I liked Virgie. A lot. She was little, littler than me. And when you're a guy and you're only five feet and two fuckin' inches tall, little girls are sweet. Really sweet. And Virgie was. I didn't even have to be funny around Virgie. She liked me for me. Whatever that is. We got away together one night. Away from the gang—her brother and the rest of them punks. And we went over to St. Matt's."

I sat quietly, realizing Joey had forgotten I was there. Somewhere inside of me there's this maternal instinct I've rarely put to use. It was coming out now. Poor little Joey, part of me was thinking.

"There's this little chapel around the back," he said, "got a little cemetery there, real old one. The chapel used to be used for funerals for that little cemetery, back in the old days. But nobody used the chapel for that no more. It'd been deconsecrated and the church just used it for storage of old shit nobody cared about. I knew about it 'cause I'd been an altarboy at St. Matt's when I was twelve. For about a fuckin' week. So me and Virgie went there one night. To be alone. I didn't plan nothing, really. I brought a rubber along just in case, but I really didn't plan nothing. But we started making out. It woulda been my first time. I was fourteen. Virgie was thirteen. It woulda been her first time, too."

He was quiet for so long I thought he'd fallen asleep. I started to get up to throw a cover over him, when his voice started up again.

"But then Reggie and the others found us. And

they beat the shit out of me. I mean, they really did. They beat me so bad I was in the hospital for two weeks. Mouth wired shut, broken arm, rib punctured a lung. I was in real bad shape. Almost died. When my old man found out about Virgie, her being a nigger and all, he woulda beat me up himself, 'cept I was already messed up so bad he couldn't find a place on me to break that wasn't already broke.

"So, when I got out, he sent me to live with his cousin Mario in Southie in Boston. Oh, yeah, Pops, smooth move. Southie in the sixties was a real class place to send an Eye-tie." Joey sighed. "Next time I got to Brooklyn, that Christmas to see the family, Virgie was already on her way to having her first kid, with some nigger friend of Reggie's. And she was only thirteen. She got married two kids later. To the same guy. I just heard this. I never seen her again. Not since that night her brother beat me up."

Joey stopped talking then. In a few minutes, a gentle snore rose from my bed. I got one of the extra blankets and spread it over him. I took the other and spread it over me on the love seat and went to sleep.

The next time I woke up to hammering on my door, it was ten o'clock. I staggered to the door and opened it. I forgot I hadn't replaced the chain since Joey came in. Pucci stood on my threshold. "So, thought you might like to hear the information I got last night," he said, moving past me into the room. He stopped short when he saw Joey in my bed.

He looked at Joey, then looked at me. "Well, at

least I know it's not because I'm Italian," he said, then walked out the door.

I closed the door behind him and leaned on it. Out loud I said, "I'm in the middle of a frigging romance novel!"

9

got dressed and, leaving Joey snoring away in my bed, went downstairs. Pucci was in the dining room with Max. I stood there for a minute, behind Pucci, listening to battling ethnic slurs. The two were obviously becoming best buddies.

Finally, during a lull in the merriment, I said, "Pucci, got a minute?"

Max waved and left and I took a seat at the table with Pucci and his cup of coffee. "What?" he said.

"I'm not *even* gonna dignify your reaction upstairs with an explanation. . . ."

"Lady, like I could care who you sleep with—"

"Don't start with me, Pucci."

We sat there and glared at each other. Finally, Pucci said, "Well, was he any good?"

I stood up. "The best I've ever had." I walked away from the table.

Pucci caught me by the arm at the door to the lobby. "Don't get your knickers in a knot, Kruse. If I really thought you'd sleep with that little jerk, I'd take my gun out right now and shoot you. Just in case you didn't use birth control. We Italian Catholics may not believe in abortion, but murder's another story."

"Perpetuating stereotypes again, are we, Pucci?"

"What's he doing in your room?"

"He wanted to convince me he didn't kill anybody so I'd convince you. Since he seems to think I have so much influence over you."

"Whatever would give him that idea?"

"I haven't the faintest notion." I leaned against the doorjamb and looked at him. Ten-thirty in the morning and the poor guy needed a shave. I wondered if he had hair on his back. I wouldn't like that. At least, I didn't think I would. "Pucci," I said, the words coming from somewhere other than my head, "are you married?"

"In the eyes of the church and in the eyes of my mother," he said. "But my wife's husband doesn't think so."

"Kids?"

"Two. Frankie, fifteen, and Anthony, twelve."

"Both boys?"

"Yes."

"Do you see them often?"

"Not enough. Every other weekend, two weeks in the summer, and every other holiday."

"Do they live here in Chicago?"

He shook his head. "In a suburb."

We looked at each other. He really had great

eyes. And they weren't so high up that I couldn't look right in them. I mentally shook myself like a dog after a dip, and said, "So what did you learn last night?"

He gestured toward the table, where his coffee was getting cold. "Let me buy you a cup of coffee," he said, "and I'll tell all."

"As long as two fried eggs, some sausage, hash browns, and toast go with the coffee."

"Jesus, you eat more than anybody I've ever seen."

"I have a high metabolism."

We walked to the table and sat down. Max came over and we ordered. "You're only gonna eat a sweet roll?" I said in mock horror after Pucci had ordered.

"I need the sugar rush after last night."

"So what happened?"

"Everybody claimed to have an alibi for the murders in Oregon and Battle Creek. Except Scarlotti. He happened to be in Battle Creek on the night in question. Was even working with the guy who bought it. And," he said, "another interesting insight—Babe Marsh happened to have worked with Don Resson before. And with Mike Burley. Both on the same night."

I looked at him. There was another shoe to drop, I could tell. But he was taking his sweet time letting it go.

Pucci grinned. "It happened to be the same night she worked with Cab Neusberg."

"No shit?" I said, excitement building.

"And . . ."

"What? What!"

"Guess who was emcee?"

I sat back in my chair, unable to drink my coffee. "Mickey Reynolds."

"The one and only."

"Who else was on the bill?"

"A guy named Gary Baker and another woman named Lorette Binz. You know them?"

I nodded. "I worked with Lorette in Canada at a women's comedy club. And Gary's from Texas. We used to work together a lot on the circuit down there." I gulped some coffee. "Are they okay?"

"I tracked them both down through their agents first thing this morning. Both alive and well. And both with audiences for alibis for most of the murders."

"What's going on? Do you think Babe . . ."

Pucci shook his head. "I'm not yet in a position to point a finger at anybody. But we're certainly checking out her alibis. She says she was at a club in Maine when Resson got hit by the car and she was supposedly at her mother's in Cincinnati, Ohio, when the guy in Battle Creek bought it. So—"

"What about Rea Carmody and Bucky Schwartz?" I asked.

"The Carmody is alibied out the butt. She was on two long-distance calls and in conference— simultaneously—with three Japanese businessmen during the Oregon incident and was on a plane in midair during the Battle Creek murder. She was also on the phone with a guy in Cleveland during the time the ME feels Mickey Reynolds was getting his."

"That was in the middle of the night. The ME

said somewhere between midnight and eight A.M., right?"

"Yeah." He grinned. "The guy in Cleveland wasn't real happy to be talking to her at that time of night, I can assure you."

"She's got that cellular phone. . . ."

"Right. She was carrying on a conversation about shares and points while breaking Mickey Reynolds's neck. She's cool, honey, but not that cool."

I ignored the fact that he'd unconsciously called me by an endearment. It happens. It meant nothing. So why did I want to rub his leg with my foot under the table?

"What about the old Buckmeister?" I asked.

Pucci took a sip of new coffee and swallowed. "Different story altogether. We can't find His Schwartzness."

"What do you mean you can't find him?"

The eyebrow went up. "Did I stutter?"

"Did you look in the trailer behind the comedy club?"

"Of course. He's not there. The Carmody has no idea where he is either. We called his apartment in New York but his roommate hasn't heard from him since the morning after Cab got killed."

"When was the last time anybody saw him?"

He shrugged. "I haven't gotten around to asking that. I just found out about an hour ago that we can't find him." He paused. "So, Ms. Kruse, when was the last time you saw Bucky Schwartz?"

I thought back. He'd spent the afternoon after Cab's death trying to accuse me of killing his boss. That's the last communication I remembered with him. "I guess that afternoon. When he left with you for his interview," I told Pucci.

He finished the last piece of sweet roll and stood up. "I guess I'd better get over to the Carlton and find out if anyone's seen him since."

"Don't forget Joey's up in my room."

"Now how could I forget that?" he asked.

Joey was snoring away when I got back upstairs. Deciding to let him sleep, I went out on a well-deserved shopping spree. I needed more clothes if I was going to stay in Chicago for a few more days. I'd only packed enough for three. And those three were up. I needed underwear and something to lift my spirits. I found the underwear at the mall. My spirits were lifted at a little boutique in the off part of downtown by a patchwork jacket of strips of kid-glove leather and raw silk in black and white, with a pattern of mauve wood roses with black leaves on a white background, handmade by underpaid, exploited peasants in Sri Lanka. They wanted three hundred and seventy-five dollars for it. I only wanted to spent two hundred. We compromised at three seventy-five. Plus tax. Two hundred and eighty topped off my Visa card, I paid six dollars in cash, and they took a check for the remainder. So I wouldn't eat in May.

On the way out of the store I was struck dumb by a pair of glow-in-the-dark boxer shorts you wouldn't believe. A black background covered with Easter bunnies and decorated eggs in loud Day-Glo colors. I paid ten bucks in cash for those, putting them in my purse for when the urge hit to stand out in the dark.

I wore the jacket out of the store and went to the movies to see *Scent of a Woman*. It was a totally unconscious move on my part. Not too far into the movie it dawned on me I was looking at what Pucci would look like in ten to fifteen years. The realization caused me to spill Coke on the sleeve of the brand-new jacket.

On the way back to the hotel, I took the jacket to the dry cleaner's. I got back to my room at five o'clock. My bed was made and there was no note from Joey Scarlotti. It was just as well. He probably wouldn't be real happy with me when he remembered telling me about his lady love.

And I had to think about that. Joey Scarlotti had to be in his late thirties to early forties. And the last true love of his life was when he was fourteen? The last woman he related to was almost thirty years ago? It was incredibly sad. It was also incredibly suspicious. What kind of sicko had that big a problem relating to women? The kind of sicko that could kill other comics for . . . whatever reason? Maybe. I had, without really thinking about it, mentally discarded him as a suspect simply because I felt sorry for him. But he'd had access to Cab. He also had had access to the comic in Battle Creek. And who—besides the Carmody—would have a cast-iron alibi from twelve to eight A.M. on the morning Mickey Reynolds was killed?

I decided to put off thinking about Joey and stuff my face instead. It had practically been hours since the popcorn, Coke, and red-hots at the movies. I went downstairs and ordered the deluxe dinner—T-bone steak, baked potato with the works, a salad, dinner rolls, and blueberry cobbler.

The Carmody walked into the dining room carrying a briefcase just as I finished the cobbler. I had to hope the blueberries hadn't stained my teeth as I smiled a greeting at her.

She sat down at my table without preamble. "Bucky Schwartz is missing," she said.

"So I heard."

"Do you know where he is?" she asked.

"If I knew, I would have told Detective Pucci when *he* asked me."

"I, for one, don't think you killed Cab," she said.

"Thank you," I said. "I don't think I did either."

The phone rang as she was giving me a quizzical look. The phone in her briefcase. She picked up the case, popped the latches, and took out the cellular phone.

"Carmody."

She listened for about a minute, then said, "Well, roll it over." In an exasperated tone of voice, she said, "Into bonds. Municipal. Kansas City's at seven-point-five right now. If Consolidated splits, we'll go back. But not until." She blew into the phone. "Are you listening to me? I said now." She hung up and looked at me. She smiled. It didn't touch her eyes. "Business," she said.

I really hadn't confused it with pillow talk. "Why are you here?" I asked her.

"To see if you knew where Bucky was," she said.

"Why didn't you just call?"

"I was in the neighborhood. . . ."

"In this neighborhood?" I asked.

Rea Carmody sighed and leaned back in the

cracked-vinyl-covered chair. "I just wanted to get a good look at you," she said.

"At me?"

"To see who Cab dumped me for," she said.

Ah-ha, I thought, the plot thickens. "I'm sorry," I said. "I didn't know. . . ."

She waved my words away with her hand. "It was really no big deal. He was great in the sack and I would have liked it to last a little longer. I don't like being dumped. I'm usually the dumper—not the dumpee."

Could she really hate being dumped so much that she'd kill Cab—then what about the others? Had she been sleeping with all of them? I had been a semidecent medical malpractice insurance investigator. But I was beginning to think I was out of my depth on murder.

"Does Detective Pucci know about this?" I finally asked.

She smiled. Again, there was no cause to worry about crow's-feet. "Of course. Would I tell you if it was a secret I was keeping from the police?"

So why hadn't Pucci told me? Was he protecting me, the creep? Worrying about my gentle, female sensibilities?

"Could I buy you a cup of coffee?" I asked.

The Carmody touched one long, crimson-nailed finger to the surface of the table, leaving a streak in the grease. She wrinkled her aquiline nose. "I think not," she said.

I suppressed an overwhelming urge to lick the tabletop and decided to pump her instead. Bert Kaiser seemed to know a lot about her business. I wondered just how much she knew about his.

"Have you known Bert long?" I asked.

"Bert?" she laughed. "Interesting segue."

"Well," I said, tracing the grease on the tabletop with my finger, "he mentioned you the other day. Talked about what a wonderful business manager you are."

"I'm not taking on any new clients right now," she said quickly. Too quickly. Like she thought I'd want her as my business manager. Pa—leeze!

"Oh, no," I said smiling, "I'm quite happy with my current people. I'm just interested in what you think of the Kaiser Komedy Klub. Whether, in your professional opinion, it's going to make a go of it."

She smiled an I-know-so-much-it's-disgusting kind of smile and said, "Bert's like the little boy looking through the pile of manure because he knows there's got to be a pony in there someplace. But optimistic as he may be, he's still realistic enough to back himself up three ways from breakfast."

"You're implying he's not the sole owner of the comedy club?"

She smiled "Who is the sole owner of anything these days?"

I thought about my new jacket that Visa and I jointly owned. Maybe she was right. I decided to take a stab in the dark. "I've gotten the impression that Bert's silent partners might be—" I put my finger on my nose and bent it sideways.

She laughed. "Why would organized crime want anything to do with a comedy club? Most of the types running the clubs these days are idiots who've run bars or titty clubs and have decided comedy's a lucrative business."

Inwardly, I agreed. These were the guys who all of a sudden decided they were experts on who is good enough to work their clubs and what position the poor bozos will work—opener, middle, or headliner. The kind of guys who say, "Now that's funny," without cracking a smile.

"No," the Carmody said, still smiling in that condescending way she seemed partial to that made me want to dislocate certain crucial facial bones. "I doubt organized crime would be interested in Bert's little club. Admittedly, Bert is better able to run a club than the other types I mentioned, having been in the comedy business for as long as he has, but still, I doubt his club would ever make enough money to interest that type, even as a laundry."

"Then who is backing him?" I asked bluntly.

"Bert's investors are none of my business. Or yours, I would think."

Just then, Max motioned to me from behind the lunch counter.

"Kimster, telephone," he said, holding the receiver of the white princess aloft.

Rea Carmody stood. "Well," she said, "I need to be going anyway."

"Nice of you to drop by," I said.

We shook hands, or I should say she offered me the tips of her fingers to shake, and she left. On the way to the phone, though, I had to wonder why she had shown up at all.

"Hello?" I said into the receiver.

"Kimmey?"

"Yes?"

"Hi, it's Babe Marsh."

Oh boy, I thought. "Well, hey, Babe," I said, "how you doing?"

"I'm getting a little antsy, Kimmey, if you want to know the truth. Just sitting around this hotel room until your detective says we can go."

My detective. Pucci would love that. "I know what you mean," I said.

"Would you like to do something?" Babe asked. "A movie? Dinner? Something like that?"

Dinner. Naw. Probably shouldn't. "I've already eaten, but a movie sounds good. Anything but *Scent of a Woman*. I saw that this afternoon."

"Well, why don't you come on over here? I haven't eaten and I'll get room service to send something up and I'll check the paper for a movie somewhere within walking distance."

"Sounds great," I said. "I'll see you in about thirty minutes."

It was cool outside so I put on the Greenbay Junior High letter jacket since my genuine exploited-worker jacket was in the cleaners, and, armed with my Chicago Transit Authority guidebook, bussed it to the Carlton.

The place was jumping with ad execs, district managers, and stockbrokers as I made my way through the crowd to the elevator. On the four-teenth floor, I turned, heading for 1423. It was right outside her door that I heard the crash. Then Babe's scream cut short. I threw my shoulder at the lock of her door, bounced off it, and hit the wall on the other side of the hall. So much for Kimmey Kruse, girl detective.

was sitting on the floor nursing my shoulder when I heard Babe scream again. Then the sound of something else crashing to the floor. I jumped to my feet and began yelling.

"Fire!" I yelled, banging on Babe's door. "Fire!"

A few people wandered into the hall from their rooms, confused, annoyed, curious. "Call hotel security!" I yelled at one man standing nearby. He looked at his companion, a blond who didn't appear to be anybody's wife, and slinked back into his room, shutting and locking his door behind the two of them.

"Somebody call the damn cops now!" I yelled.

A gray-haired woman who resembled my ninth-grade algebra teacher said, "I've already called downstairs. Security is on their way up. Is there really a fire or were you just trying to get some attention?''

She walked toward me as she spoke, where I still stood at Babe's door, hammering. "My friend's been hurt," I said.

"Are you sure?" she asked.

"She screamed twice and there was the sound of furniture breaking. . . .''

"Stand back, dear," the reincarnation of my algebra teacher said, moving me aside with one long arm. She lifted her sensible-length skirt above her knee, raised her sensible-shoe-clad foot, and kicked the door right above the doorknob. There was a splintering sound but nothing happened. She kicked one more time, and the door flew open.

I ran around her into the room. The door to the balcony was open, the curtains blowing in the room from the hurricane winds Chicago calls a spring breeze. A standing lamp was turned over on the floor, the light still burning, casting weird shadows around the room. The love seat was on its side, and behind it I could see one large foot sticking out.

I ran around the love seat, the algebra teacher close behind. Babe lay in a very large heap on the floor, blood from a head wound pooling on the thick beige carpet.

"I didn't do anything," I said, slinking down further on the plastic seat of the emergency-room waiting area.

The large, automatic double doors of the entrance opened and shut continually with the stream of sick and injured coming through them. Some came on foot, some on gurneys, some stand-

ing and being dragged by friends and loved ones.
The cold night air came in with them and I shivered
in my lightweight football jacket.

The waiting room was packed. A Hispanic family took up two rows of chairs, a mother, several
children, some grandchildren, possibly an aunt or
two.

A black man sat beside me, his wife beside him,
helping him hold a bloody washcloth to his forehead.

"I tole you the nex' time . . ." she began.

"But, honey, I wasn't doin' nothin' . . ."

"Well, you do nothin' away from that ho', you
got me?" she said and slapped him hard on the leg.

He groaned and looked longingly at the people
being rushed in ahead of him.

A young white couple sat on the other side of
Pucci, the young woman holding a very still, very
quiet infant.

"I didn't do anything," I told Pucci.

"I know," he said, sighing, "but you're always
there when somebody else does."

"I can't help that."

"Yes you can," he said. "You can lock yourself
in your room or leave town."

"You told me not to."

"I lied. I want you to leave town. Actually, I'd
prefer it if you left the country. As soon as they start
taking names for the shuttle, you could accommo-
date me by—"

"Shut up, Pucci," I said with a sigh. He was
making me tired. Of course, everything was making me tired. And hungry.

Babe was alive. That much we knew. How alive

or for how long, no one was telling. She had been semiconscious when we found her, but hadn't said anything distinguishable. She'd passed out when the paramedics had attempted to lift her. It had taken the three paramedics, the two men from hotel security, and Pucci to get her onto the stretcher and to get the stretcher down to the ambulance. The fact that that was the exact same number of people usually used as pallbearers entered my mind. I have one of *those* kinds of minds.

Pucci took my hand in his, his fingers playing with the silver legs of the spider ring on my left index finger. His finger ran over the bloodred garnet that served as the spider's body. "Ugly ring," he said.

"Thank you," I said.

"You dress weird."

"You dress like you have a charge card at Sears," I said.

"I do."

"I'm not surprised."

He looked down at my feet, at the cowboy boots with black leather toes and imitation unborn-calf-skin uppers, adorned at the top with three red cowbells each. (I'd taped the clappers. I mean, they're cute, but the noise is annoying.)

"Where do you buy something like that?" he asked.

"You don't. These were handmade for me by a gifted and talented friend. An artist."

He snorted.

"So what happened to Babe?" I asked.

Pucci shrugged. "We're not sure. A couple two stories down from Babe's room experienced coitus interruptus when some guy came barrelling in through their balcony door and out their front door, but they didn't get a good look at him because they had the lights off—"

"How ordinary of them."

"—and as far as we can tell, he got out of the building. I've got men doing a room-to-room, but I don't expect to find anything."

It seemed to me somebody was after the people who had played in Atlanta six months before. I couldn't help thinking of the two comedians left, both friends of mine: Gary Baker from Texas, a tall, lanky guy with a deep drawl who got more laughs from looking at the audience than most comedians get with their whole set, and Lorette Binz, a funny, gentle, crazy Canadian.

"What about Gary and Lorette?" I asked.

"Gary's at home in Houston and I called the HPD and informed them of what's going on. They're putting a squad car in front of his house for a little while. Couple of days, maybe. But that's all they can spare."

"And Lorette?"

"We can't find her."

"Oh, shit," I said, slumping down further in my seat.

He reached over and touched my hair, his hand gently caressing my new perm. "Don't worry. She's between gigs. On the road, they think. Somewhere between Akron and Pittsburgh. She'll be checking in tonight with the guy she's living with in Ontario. He says she calls every other day, and today's the day for her to call."

I leaned my head back against the wall, accidently squashing Pucci's hand between the wall and my head. "Oops," I said, leaning forward as he tried to retrieve his hand.

"That's okay," he said. "For some reason, I expect pain from you." He rubbed his hand and stood up. "I'm gonna go check on Babe."

I started to get up too, but Pucci shook his head. "Just stay put. I'll bring back some coffee. How do you take yours?"

"Double cream and double sugar," I said.

"Why did I know that?" he muttered as he walked down the hall, rubbing his injured hand. Actually, making a pretty big deal out of it. Like my head's big enough to actually *hurt* his stupid hand!

I leaned my head against the wall again, not hurting anyone this time, and thought about what could possibly be happening. I needed to sort this out. I needed to talk it out. The only way I knew to do that was with Phoebe. I got up and went to a nearby pay phone and dialed zero and Phoebe's ten digits, then the fourteen digits of my calling-card number, naturally memorized.

Phoebe picked up on the second ring. "Okay," I said. "How many dead did we have last time I called you?"

"What?"

"Try to follow along, Phoeb."

"Two. Cab and that emcee person."

"Try four and one on hold," I said.

"What are you talking about?"

So I told her about the murders in Oregon and Battle Creek and the attempt on Babe's life, and the connection to the gig they'd all done together in Atlanta six months before.

"Whoa," she said. "This is getting hairy."

"So? What? Somebody didn't feel they got their money's worth at Atlanta? What?"

"I have no idea. I don't exactly have a psychopathic mind, Kimmey. If I did, Nathaniel would have been chopped up in little pieces long ago."

"Woulda worked for me," I said.

"Who are you talking to?"

I turned. Pucci was standing behind me, foam coffee cups in his hands. "Those aren't biodegradable, you know," I said, taking one of the cups.

"Who are you talking to?" Phoebe asked.

"Pucci," I said into the phone. "My friend in Austin. The lawyer. Phoebe," I said to Pucci.

"Let me talk to him," Phoebe said.

"What?"

"Let . . . me . . . talk . . . to . . . him!" she repeated succinctly.

I handed the phone to Pucci. "She wants to talk to you, for some strange reason."

I stood back and listened unabashedly. Which, I must admit, is my style.

"Oh, yeah, she was there this time, too," Pucci said into the phone. I hate one-sided phone calls, but I knew Phoebe well enough to know part of what was being said.

"I'm thinking about putting a bell around her neck," Pucci said. He listened for a minute and then laughed uproariously. "You're right," he said. "Boy, are you right!"

I was getting madder by the minute. The fact that they were discussing yours truly was not lost on me. When Pucci turned and looked at me, an expression of surprise on his face, I knew Phoebe had gone too far.

"No kidding?" Pucci said.

That's when I grabbed the phone. "Go!" I said to Pucci, pointing toward the chairs where we'd been sitting. To Phoebe, I said, "What did you say?"

"When?"

"Phoebe!"

"Look, Kimmey, I've got to run. The dryer buzzer just went off and all my permanent press are in there. You *know* what happens if you ignore a dryer buzzer! Bye!"

And she was gone. Just like that. The bitch.

I went over and stood in front of Pucci. "How's Babe?" I asked.

He shook his head. "The same. Unconscious but not necessarily in a coma, according to the docs."

I heaved a sigh. Was that good news? Was that bad news? Or was that no news at all?

"They're moving her out of ER to a room upstairs," Pucci said, standing. "There's a waiting room on the unit. We can do what we're doing as well up there as here."

"Yeah, I suppose," I said, following him down the hall and out of ER to the entrance to the hospital and a row of elevators.

We got on and he pushed a button for the eighth floor.

"What did Phoebe say to you?" I asked as we rode upward.

"About what?"

"Pucci!"

He raised that eyebrow. "She was just giving me her legal expertise on the case, that's all."

"Bull. She's a corporate attorney."

"And a very intelligent one, too."

"You two were talking about me!"

Pucci shook his head. "You know, that's the thing about paranoids. The incredible ego!"

The door opened on eight and I turned on my three-inch cowboy-boot heels and walked across the empty waiting room to the row of chairs on the other side, sat down, and glared at Pucci, who had taken a seat and was leaning his head against the wall, his eyes closed, whistling soundlessly. What a jerk.

I awoke with a start, Pucci's hand on my shoulder. Glancing at my antique Spiro Agnew watch, I saw it was somewhere between three and four A.M. It's never been real good about keeping time, but then I've never been real good about wanting to know the time.

"What?" I managed to get out between the cotton balls in my mouth.

"Babe's awake," Pucci said.

I leaned my head against the wall, tears filling my eyes. "Thank God," I said.

He held out his hand to help me up. "Have you talked with her?" I asked him.

He shook his head, leading me down the hall. "I tried. But she kept asking if you were okay. I told her you were but she wouldn't believe me. Come on in and show her."

We got to Babe's room and I tentatively stuck my head inside. "Babe?" I called softly.

She turned her head toward the sound of my voice and her face began to crumple. "Oh, Kimmey!"

I moved inside quickly and sat down in the chair next to her bed, taking the hand without the IV tube in mine. Pucci stood in the doorway watching us. "It's okay, Babe. I'm fine. *You're* the one everybody's been worried about!"

"I have a headache," she said.

"I'm not surprised," I said, rubbing the back of her hand. "You got hit on the head."

"Oh, goodness." She reached up to touch her head and found only bandages. "My hair!"

I looked at Pucci. I had no idea what was under the bandages. He walked all the way into the room and patted Babe on the shoulder. "It's okay. They only had to shave a small spot in the back where you got hit. The hair on top will cover that while it's growing back. They didn't bother your pretty hair."

I looked up into Pucci's eyes and smiled. Maybe he wasn't a total bastard.

"Okay," Babe said, leaning back against her pillows. "May I have an aspirin?"

"We'll check with the nurse on our way out, okay?" I said.

"Okay," Babe agreed.

Pucci sat down at the foot of Babe's bed and patted her leg. "I know you might not feel quite up to this, Ms. Marsh, but I need to ask you a few questions. Just until you get too tired, okay?"

"I guess."

"Did you see who attacked you?" Pucci asked.

Babe looked at me then away from both of us. "No, I don't think so."

"Can you remember anything?" Pucci asked. "The balcony door opening? Anything?"

Babe shook her head, unable to look at either of us. I hadn't known Babe all that long, but I did know when she was lying. Which was now. I rubbed her hand again. "Babe, you have to tell us the truth. We don't want anything else to happen to you. Or to Gary Baker or Lorette Binz."

Babe looked at me, a frown on her ample face. "What? What are you talking about?"

"Whoever did this to you we're pretty sure is the same one who killed Cab, Mickey Reynolds, Don Resson, and Mike Burley. The one thing all of you have in common is the gig in Atlanta. And Gary and Lorette were there, too. They could be next."

"Oh, my goodness. Oh, my goodness." Babe closed her eyes and leaned her head back. "I'm not sure. I didn't get a real good look at him, and I'd only met him twice before, but . . ."

She opened her eyes and looked first at me then at Pucci. Heaving a great sigh, she said, "I think it was Bucky Schwartz."

It was seven o'clock in the morning and Pucci and I were sharing the dining room at the Lake House with blue-collar workers on their way to the job. It had been a long night. We'd left Babe's room a little after four (according to Pucci's watch), after he'd arranged to have a uniformed officer sit outside her room, and had gone straight to the police station. I'd slept on the way over there, then, once inside, had managed, despite the noise of a Chicago PD squad room in the wee hours of the morning (which appeared to be just as noisy as the same Chicago PD squad room had sounded in the middle of the afternoon), to find a chair to curl up in and sleep some more.

My metabolism being what it is, I desperately need at least eight hours of sleep a day. Luckily, I can take my eight hours in little spurts and still manage to walk and talk with the living.

Pucci woke me up at about six-thirty and dragged me back out to the squad car, where I slept again until we were in the dining room of the Lake House. Hunger won out over sleep at that point. Hunger and curiosity.

"So, what did you accomplish while I was sleeping?" I asked him, looking at the three days' growth of beard that had miraculously appeared in just a couple of hours, the red-rimmed eyes, the messy hair. I grinned. He looked like hell.

"What are you grinning about?"

"You look like hell."

"Thanks. On the other hand, you look like you've just walked out of a refreshing shower."

"Is that sarcasm?"

Pucci sighed. "I wish it was. Actually, you do look great."

Jeeze. Endearments. Compliments. And he hadn't tried to arrest me for hours. Maybe it was love. "Thank you," I finally managed to say. "So, what did you accomplish?"

"I put out an APB on Bucky Schwartz and on Lorette Binz. We need to find her now. She didn't call her boyfriend last night. I had to wake him up to find that out, but there it is."

"Oh, shit."

"Yeah. Oh, shit. So, we're looking for her. We're looking for him. And we've got Gary Baker under house arrest in Houston and he is not a, excuse the expression, happy camper."

"I'm sorry. I don't excuse that expression. Ever."

"Did you hear about the seven dwarfs and their audience with the pope?" Pucci asked.

I turned to Max, who was balancing breakfast trays and heading for a table of four guys who had their names sewn on their pockets. "Oh, Max, it's for you!"

"Be right there!" he called back.

"You're too good to listen to my joke?" Pucci asked, a scowl on his face.

"Yes," I answered, "I am."

He leaned forward. "Well, I'm gonna tell it to you anyway and when you go on Letterman and this is the only thing you can remember, I'm going to laugh my ass off."

"And it was such a cute little ass," I said.

Pucci looked over his shoulder at the thing he sat on. "Yeah?"

I sighed. "Don't get all bent out of shape. It was just an expression."

"Funny. I've never heard that expression. How does it go again?"

Max made it to the table and sat down, attempting to steal a rasher of bacon from my plate. I slapped his hand and he took one off of Pucci's instead. "You beckoned, Princess Kimster?"

"The idiot thinks he has a joke to tell."

The idiot smiled at me. "Honey, you better watch it. I'll be taking your gigs in no time flat."

I yawned. "I'm worried, Pucci. Watch me worry."

He turned to Max. "Okay. The seven dwarfs have an audience with the pope . . ."

"Which pope?" I asked.

Pucci glared at me. "There's only one pope."

"Spoken like a true Catholic. But I mean, at what time? Are we talking present-day pope or a pope from days gone by? Because, if I remember my fairy tale correctly, the seven dwarfs were back in, well, some other time period, wouldn't you say, Max?"

Ignoring me, Pucci said, "And the pope was reading them Scriptures . . ."

"Which Scriptures? I mean, I wonder what Scriptures would be appropriate to read to people named Dopey and Sneezy and Doc and—"

Max's hand went over my mouth. It tasted slightly of Mr. Clean.

"—and Dopey raises his hand in the air and says, 'Sir, do you have any dwarf nuns in Alaska?' And the pope says, 'No, Dopey, I'm sorry we don't.' He starts to read again and Dopey raises his hand and says, 'Sir, are there any dwarf nuns in the Northern Hemisphere?' and the pope says, 'No, Dopey, I'm sorry, there are no dwarf nuns in the Northern Hemisphere.'"

I bit Max's hand and he yelled and pulled it away. "I'll be good," I said. "I'll sit here quietly, eating my breakfast. I won't interrupt. I won't say a word, I swear—"

"Shut up!" Pucci said. I shut up. To Max he said, "How long have you known this brat?"

"Entirely too long. Finish the story."

"So the pope says no dwarf nuns in the Northern Hemisphere, right? Okay. So he starts reading the Scriptures again. Dopey interrupts again and says, 'Sir, are there any dwarf nuns anywhere in the world?' And the pope says, 'No, Dopey, I'm sorry, but there are no dwarf nuns anywhere in the whole world.' So all the other dwarfs start laughing like crazy and say, 'Dopey fucked a penguin! Dopey fucked a penguin!' ''

Max laughed and I glared. "That's it?" I demanded. "That's funny to you people?"

"Okay," Pucci said. "You be funny. I dare you."

"I don't do breakfast crowds, thank you very much."

"You mean you can't do breakfast crowds. Or even on demand," Pucci said.

I was always the one Phoebe dared to do things because I'd always do them. It has gotten me into a lot of trouble over the years.

I stood up and walked to the nearest empty table, pulled out a chair, stepped on it and then up to the table. I smiled. "Hi, folks, glad ya'll could make it this morning. . . ."

I walked into Babe's room with an armful of spring flowers fresh from the florist. Daisies and daffodils, iris and black-eyed Susans, peonies and tulips. Babe's eyes got huge.

"Oh, Kimmey! They're beautiful!"

"Hi, Babe, how you doing?" I asked, scrounging around the room for a vase.

"Here," Babe said, handing me her plastic water pitcher. "Put them in here. They're just lovely!"

I smiled. "I'm glad you like 'em. Nothing cheers up a room more than spring flowers. But you know, I couldn't find a bluebonnet to save my life in this damn town."

"Next time, then, I'll get hit in the noggin in Texas, okay?"

I sat down on the chair next to the bed. "You

must be feeling better," I said. "You are crackin' wise. That's a good sign."

Babe sighed heavily. "Oh, Kimmey, I feel so bad about saying it was Bucky that did this. What if I'm wrong? I'm mean, I could be. I really could."

"When Pucci's men find him, we'll find out if you're right or wrong."

"But what if Detective Pucci wants me to pick him out of a lineup? I don't think I could do it."

I patted her hand. "We'll worry about that when the time comes."

"Are Gary and Lorette still okay?"

I sighed my own sigh. "Gary's okay. But they can't find Lorette."

Babe sat up quickly. "Oh, my God!"

I patted her hand. "Lie down, now. You be good or I'll sic one of those nasty-looking nurses on you." Babe lay back on her pillows while I stroked her hand. "Lorette probably just couldn't get to a phone last night, that's all. They'll find her and she'll be fine."

"I hope so," Babe whispered.

"Look, how could he be busting your head in Chicago and doing anything to Lorette somewhere between Akron, Ohio, and Pittsburgh, PA? Huh? Answer me that."

Babe sighed. Finally, she smiled faintly. "You're right."

"Now, tell me everything you know about Bucky Schwartz. Was he in Atlanta when you and Cab were both there?"

"Oh, yes. He was there. Running around getting things for Cab. Diet Coke, mostly."

"Did anything happen there that could, I don't

know, shed some light on this? Like maybe Cab bawled him out or took his girlfriend, or something like that?''

"Not that I saw," Babe answered. "You might ask that woman, what's her name, Rea Carmody?''

I sat back in my chair and looked at Babe. "Rea Carmody was in Atlanta?''

"Didn't I mention that?''

"No, Babe, not to me." I jumped up and headed for the door. "I'll be back later!''

"Why the hell didn't she say Carmody was there to begin with?'' Pucci said, swerving between cars.

"Because she'd just been hit on the head, dumb butt. I think she did real good, considering!''

We were in Pucci's personal car—a 1972 Chevy Impala three-tone, brown, tan, and primer gray. I was sitting on a beach towel with a giant head of Snoopy on it that tried valiantly to cover the springs and other nasty things coming out of the holes in the upholstery. It failed miserably. With every bump—and there were plenty, what with the number of potholes in the greater Chicago street system averaging about a zillion per—part of my butt sank into the holes in the upholstery and part was being punctured by a spring.

"Well, if Carmody's dead, Babe Marsh is gonna get an earful from me," Pucci said.

"I don't remember you asking her if Carmody was in Atlanta."

"I didn't ask her if Donald Trump was in Atlanta, either."

"You're splitting hairs, Pucci."

He pulled up with a squeal of tires in front of a

high-rise apartment complex and both of us jumped out of the car.

"Why didn't we just call?" I asked.

"Because the line was busy," he answered.

"Sounds like business as usual to me."

"If you wanted to kill Carmody and make it look like she was okay, wouldn't you take the phone off the hook to make it look like she was talking to Timbuktu?"

Since I had just recently been taken off the number-one-suspect list, I didn't think it prudent to answer any questions on what I would do while attempting to kill anyone.

The lobby of the Carmody's building was high-tech chrome and glass with a high-tech security guard standing "at ease" in front of the block of elevators, his arms behind his back.

"May I help you, sir?" he said to Pucci as we burst into the building.

Pucci flashed his badge. Flashing didn't work with this guy.

"May I see that, sir?" he said, holding out one hand.

Pucci handed him the little folder with the badge and ID and we stood there while he studied it. When he turned to a built-in chrome desk along the side of the lobby, obviously heading for a phone to call in and check the ID, Pucci said, "We don't have time for that. Come up with us if you want, but we think something may have happened to one of your tenants."

"Just following regulations, sir," the guy said, still heading for the phone.

"Screw this," Pucci said, grabbing the guard by

the arm. "Call Rea Carmody's apartment. See if she's okay."

The guard looked from the bank of telephones to Pucci, from Pucci to me. I nodded encouragement. Finally, he picked up a phone and dialed three digits. After almost a full minute, he said, "Ms. Carmody? There is a policeman down here. He wanted to check to see if you were all right. I haven't checked out his ID yet. . . ."

"Tell her it's Kimmey Kruse and her pet dick," I said.

The guard gulped back his laughter and repeated part of what I said. Pucci turned to me with a glare. I said, "I meant that as in detective, Pucci. Get your mind out of the gutter."

The guard looked at Pucci. "Detective Pucci?" he asked. Pucci nodded. To the phone, the guard said, "Yes, ma'am. Okay." He hung up and pointed to the bank of elevators. "The third one on the right takes you straight to the penthouse."

Ooo, penthouse. Pucci and I walked to the elevators and took the express up to the twenty-fourth floor. My ears popped and I felt slightly nauseous before we landed that thing.

The elevator opened up onto a landing with only one door leading off. That door opened almost at the same instant that the elevator doors did. Rea Carmody stood on the threshold, a phone to her ear, stocking-footed, the suit coat off, the sleeves of her silk blouse rolled up, and the bow tie of the blouse undone. The perfect picture of the busy female exec at rest. She motioned us forward.

We followed her into the foyer and then into the living room of her penthouse apartment. Since it was impossible to eavesdrop on her telephone conversation—it was in French—I checked out our surroundings instead. There were obviously some serious big bucks in personal management.

There was something about the decor, though, that was familiar. It finally dawned on me. The classic lines of the black tuxedo sofa, the black-and-white Mexican tile coffee table, the leather sling chairs, even the pictures on the walls and the knickknacks on the mantel, were straight out of an expensive local furniture-store catalog I'd recently perused. I could hear the conversation now. "Hello? This is Rea Carmody. Send one of your decorators over to my apartment. Put it on my charge."

Finally, the Carmody said "*Ciao*"—which I understood, probably because it wasn't French—and hung up.

"Well," she said, smiling at us and flinging herself down in one of the sling chairs. "What can I do for you?"

"Ms. Carmody," Pucci said as he and I took our places on the tuxedo sofa, "I just received the information that you were in Atlanta about six months ago when Cab Neusberg had a gig there, is that right?"

She looked quizzical. "Yes, that's right. Why?"

"Have you heard what happened to Babe Marsh?"

"Babe Marsh . . . Oh, that incredibly fat woman. No! Don't tell me there's been another accident!"

"It was no accident. Babe was struck on the head but her assailant wasn't able to finish the job. She's alive."

Carmody stifled a yawn. "Well, thank goodness. But what has that got to do with me?"

"Ms. Marsh has identified her assailant as Bucky Schwartz."

Carmody laughed. "You're joking, right? Bucky? Please!"

"This is no laughing matter, Ms. Carmody. So far, five of the people who were present at the gig in Atlanta have either been killed or assaulted."

"Five? Who else?"

Pucci told her about the other two, then said, "We've got a guard on Gary Baker in Texas, and an APB out on Lorette Binz. Also one on Bucky. We didn't know you'd been there, or we would have had protection for you, too."

"Whatever for? Surely no one would be after me? All these people have been comics, right? I'm certainly not a comic."

The way she said "comic" made it sound something like "booger."

"We don't know what's going on, Ms. Carmody, so for your own protection, I think it's for the best."

She shrugged. "Whatever. But why Bucky?"

"That's what I'm hoping you can tell me," Pucci said.

12

If you're expecting me to be able to tell you anything personal about Bucky, forget it. I make it a
practice to know as little as possible about the
Bucky Schwartzes of this world," the Carmody
said, leaning forward from her leather slingback
chair to reach an onyx cigarette box on the Mexican tile coffee table. She removed one of those thin,
dark brown cigarettes, about a mile of it, and lit it
with a gold Dunhill that had been lying on the
table. She drew in a breathful of smoke, exhaled,
and said, "Do you mind?"

I wanted to say yes so bad I could feel it in my
toes, but, knowing we wanted her to spill her guts,
if she had any, I just smiled and shook my head.
Waving his hand at the smoke, Pucci also, though
obviously reluctantly, nodded his agreement. As

the Carmody wasn't looking at us for our responses, I guess it didn't really matter.

"Do you know anything about his background?" Pucci asked.

Rea took another long drag and shook her head, the smoke emitting from her mouth like the trail of a steam locomotive. "Not a thing," she said, smiling. "I know his name. I know he worked for Cab. That's it."

"What exactly did he do for Cab?" I asked as Pucci shot me a look. Eyebrow down, eyes glaring. I smiled at him.

"Your typical gofer," she said, snuffing out her cigarette. "He went for, as far as I know."

"What exactly did he 'go for'?" Pucci asked. "Girls? Drugs? What?"

Carmody shrugged. "All of the above, I'm sure."

"Cab didn't do drugs," I said.

They both looked at me and Carmody laughed. "Maybe not around you, darlin'."

Okay. That was a possibility. I'm not into drugs. I tried marijuana when I was a teenager but, unfortunately, you have to smoke it and I don't smoke anything if I can help it. Later, I tried cocaine, but it made my throat numb from the top to the bottom and then made me nauseous. I got totally paranoid thinking I was going to vomit and asphyxiate because I couldn't feel anything. It was the longest, nastiest twenty minutes of my life. It was also the end of my drug experimentation. The fact that my drug of choice is alcohol was fairly well known among the people who know me and have worked with me. It was a possibility that Cab found this out so he didn't do or discuss drugs in the short time we were together.

"You're saying Neusberg did drugs?" Pucci asked.

Carmody shrugged. "No more than anyone else, I suppose. A little coke, a little weed. Just to wind down after a performance. Bucky always had a little stash of something."

"Where did he get it?" Pucci asked.

Carmody shrugged again. "I haven't the faintest idea. Like I said, Bucky was just there. To serve." She laughed.

I decided then that if I had been Bucky, the first one I would have offed would have been Rea Carmody.

"Who did Cab hire first," Pucci asked, "you or Bucky?"

Rea snorted and reached for the cigarette box again. Lighting her cancer stick, she said, "Cab didn't *hire* me, precious, we *merged,* so to speak."

"Okay," Pucci said, showing infinite patience (I would have belted her at the precious remark), "which of the two of you was *with* Neusberg first?"

"Bucky. Gofers are incredibly less expensive than business managers," Rea said, smiling and exhaling. "Poor Cab had to save up for my services."

"Did Cab ever tell you anything about Bucky?" Pucci asked.

The Carmody raised her eyebrows. "Whyever would he? I mean, it's not like we sat around discussing the hired help."

Something wasn't clicking here. It was hard to believe this was the same woman who had lowered herself to come to the Lake House to see me just because she wanted to get a closer look at the woman she was dumped for. It didn't jibe.

I stood up. "May I use your rest room?" I asked.

"Certainly," Rea said, pointing to her left. "First door on the left."

I walked down the hall, checked to see I was out of their viewing range, and headed for the last door at the end of the hall, a large double door I presumed to be the Carmody's bedroom. I was right. A chrome four-poster bed on a raised, round dais; mirrors on all walls and ceilings; a fireplace flush with the wall, the surround of brushed, shiny slate; two black, Chinese lacquered bedside tables on either side of the red-satin-draped king-size bed; and a chaise longue of black silk. I stepped into the room, sinking almost ankle deep in the plush, stark white carpet.

I thought about slipping off my shoes so as not to leave any trace of my presence, but I still had on the cowboy boots and those take twenty minutes to get off and on again. Instead, I tiptoed to the bed and quietly inched open the top right drawer on the bedside table. And found a nest of shoulder pads. All colors, all shapes, all sizes. That's all that was in there.

The bottom drawer held a box of Kleenex, a bottle of fingernail-polish remover, two emery boards, and an orange stick.

There were three obvious doors in all the mirrors. Two held enormous closets, filled to the brim with clothes. Both had built-in bureaus, shelves, shoe racks, and multilevel rods for hanging clothes. A quick look through her drawers revealed nothing. Not that I knew exactly what I was looking for.

I went to the third door, which led to the Carmody's bath.

It was huge, with a sunken tub separated from the group-sized shower stall by glass bricks. One wall was vanity—two sinks cut out of black marble with more drawers than my entire apartment has, kitchen, bathroom, and dressers combined. Makeup lights ringed the wall of mirror over the vanity. But I'll be damned if I could find a medicine cabinet. I spotted another door between the sunken tub and the wall of vanity and opened it. The johnny room.

The black enameled commode sat next to its matching black enamel bidet, and across from both was a mirror, behind which was the medicine cabinet. I opened it gingerly, and looked. All the usual. Vicks VapoRub, Extra-Strength Tylenol, a bag of Schick disposable razors, cold-sore medicine (the Carmody with herpes? Before or after Cab? I'd better check!), a prescription bottle for an antibiotic, a bottle of cough syrup with an expiration date of two years earlier, a thermometer, several boxes of Ex-Lax, and a prescription bottle of diuretics.

I heard the door to the bedroom open and quickly shut the johnny room door, pulling down my pants and sitting on the john as quickly as possible.

"Kimmey?" the Carmody called from the bathtub part of the bathroom.

"In here!" I said. "It must have been something I ate."

"You're in the wrong bathroom. I meant the one in the hall!"

I flushed, pulled up my pants, and opened the

door, allowing her to see me zip. A little authenticity, folks.

"Oh?" I said, zipping. "I'm sorry. I must have missed it."

"Come on."

She turned abruptly on her heels and marched out of the room. I followed, like the chastened puppy dog I was.

Pucci was waiting by the elevator. He turned when he heard us and held out his hand for the Carmody. "Thanks for your time, Ms. Carmody. And I'm going to call from downstairs and have a uniform sent over to guard your door."

"You really don't have to do that," she said.

Pucci smiled. "I'm afraid I must insist, Ms. Carmody. Can't have any more dead bodies popping up, now can we?"

The elevator chose that moment to arrive.

"So what did you find?" Pucci asked, buttering a Denny's dinner roll.

I gave him my innocent, wide-eyed waif look. It rarely works. "What?"

"When you searched Carmody's apartment."

"I did no such thing!" I said, working hard on my waifness.

Pucci's "Bullshit" was barely discernible between mouthfuls of dinner roll and ham steak.

"I got lost and went into the wrong bathroom, that's all."

"For fifteen minutes?"

"It must have been something I ate."

"Maybe it was everything you ate."

Having gotten a great opening to move the subject off my search, I said, "Are you intimating I eat too much?"

"I'm not *intimating* a damn thing. You're a pig. If you were a Catholic, you'd be in confession every week for the sin of gluttony."

I moved my dinner plate away from me, having finished the broiled chicken, mashed potatoes, green beans, and dinner roll in the time it took Pucci to butter his roll, and pulled the plate of apple pie toward me.

"I have a high metabolism," I said, stuffing my face with pie and ice cream.

"I hope I can see you when you reach thirty." He held his hands out away from his sides and puffed out his cheeks. "Like a balloon."

"You're jealous. And I understand perfectly. Since you've been around me, I'd say you've gained ten pounds just trying to keep up." I signaled the waitress for a refill of my Coke. And maybe just a couple more dinner rolls.

Pucci looked down at his stomach. "That's a lie. I weighed in yesterday. I'm a perfect one hundred forty. Same weight I started the academy with. I'm in perfect shape."

I reached across the table and poked the spare tire in the general vicinity of his navel. "They let you into the academy with that?"

Pucci grabbed my finger. "I've given you ample opportunity to play with it, honey."

I jerked my hand back. "You are *so* sophomoric, Pucci." I wiped my mouth delicately with my napkin. "Are you ready?"

Pucci leaned back and signaled the waitress. "A couple of coffees over here. One black. One," he looked at me and grimaced, "with double cream and double sugar."

"I'm ready to leave, Pucci."

"I'm not." He leaned forward, elbows on the table, pushing his plate toward the middle, his body hunched toward me. "So. What did you find in Carmody's apartment?"

"A nest of shoulder pads and some Vic's Vapo-Rub. The only thing I could find her guilty of is a possibility of bingeing and purging."

"What?"

I shrugged. "She had way too many boxes of Ex-Lax in her medicine cabinet and a script for diuretics. Of course, maybe she just stocked up at a drugstore sale. Who knows."

"I wonder what was in the other bedroom," Pucci mused.

"If you'd kept her busy long enough, maybe I could have found out." I leaned forward to match his body language. "Why didn't you tell me Carmody had been Cab's main squeeze before me?"

Pucci leaned back and the eyebrow shot up. "What?"

"The stuff about Cab and Rea being an item and he dumped her for me. Or something to that effect."

"Where the hell did you hear that?" The incredulity in his voice was not amusing.

"Rea told me."

"When?"

"When she came by the Lake House to see me a couple of days ago."

"About what?"

"About getting a good look at the woman Cab dumped her for."

"And you bought it?" Pucci asked.

I stood up. "Is it so impossible to believe that someone would dump la Grande Dame Carmody for little ol' me?"

"Sit down, Kruse."

"No."

"Sit down!"

I sat.

"First," Pucci said, "from what you've told me and what others have told me, you and Cab were not that hot an item. It was little more than a one-night stand. . . ."

"I don't do one-night stands!"

The eyebrow shot up.

"Okay, well, I did, but I don't."

The eyebrow went down.

"Secondly," Pucci said, "you were in the same room with her twice, right? In the green room? The first night of the gig and the day after Cab died? Right? So she didn't get a good look at you then?"

I leaned back in my chair. I knew something had been out of kilter and this was it. Carmody had lied. But why? Why did she come to the Lake House?

"What's going on?" I asked Pucci.

He signaled for the check and stood up. "That's exactly what I'm going to find out."

Back in Pucci's personal car, heading God only knew where, I asked, "Has it ever occurred to you that Bucky Schwartz may not be missing?"

Pucci looked over at me, while swerving between two cars. I let out a whoosh of air as we made it without going through anybody's windshield. "What do you mean?" he asked.

"Gary and Lorette aren't the only ones in Atlanta that haven't been accosted yet. If we can exclude Lorette. Rea Carmody appears unharmed to me."

"What are you saying?"

"What if Bucky's dead?"

"Then who belted Babe?"

"Great alliteration. I don't know. Maybe Carmody hired somebody to do it for her. Maybe she hired somebody in Battle Creek and in Oregon, too. Maybe that's why most of these murders have been done with different methods. Babe says she can't swear it was Bucky. But what if Carmody hired someone who looked vaguely like Bucky, had him dress up Buckylike, and is trying to blame all this on someone who's already dead?"

"Why?"

I shrugged. "Damned if I know. Maybe she's always had a secret desire to be a comedian but she stinks on ice and she's going around killing comics. . . ."

"Then why only the comics at that one gig in Atlanta? Why not you? Seems to me, anybody who knew you at all would want to take a swipe at you one time or another."

"*Très amusant.*"

We drove in silence. I still didn't know where we were headed. Finally, Pucci said, "Okay. Why did she come to see you at the Lake House? What exactly did she say?"

I leaned my head back against the wobbly headrest and closed my eyes, trying to remember what exactly Rea Carmody had said to me.

"She came into the dining room and told me Bucky Schwartz was missing. I said I knew. She asked if I knew where he was. She told me she didn't think I'd killed Cab. She talked on the phone for a while. . . ."

"What phone?"

I opened my eyes and glanced at Pucci. "Her cellular. She carries it in a briefcase."

"What was the phone call about?"

"Business. Roll-overs. Stuff like that."

"Okay. Then . . ."

"I asked her why she was there, she said she wanted to get a good look at me because . . . no, first she lied, said she was there to see if I knew anything about Bucky, and when I asked why she didn't just call, that's when she said . . . no, then she lied again and said she was in the neighborhood and I said, 'This neighborhood?' and she got all huffy and finally came up with that story about Cab dumping her for me. . . ."

"And you bought it."

"Screw you, Pucci."

"You gotta admit my advances to you have been of a much more refined nature, Kruse," he said.

I glared at the road ahead of me, my arms crossed over my chest. We were going down Lake Shore. The overcast sky gave the lake a grayish tinge, making it look even deader. "You know, Pucci, you're hurting my feelings," I finally said.

"I'm hurting your feelings?" he said, looking over at me.

I looked back. "Yes."

"I'm hurting your feelings?"

I looked forward and said nothing.

Pucci pulled off to the shoulder of the road and stopped the engine, turning in his seat and looking at me. His hand played with my hair while I sat looking forward, out the car window at the world going by.

"Cab Neusberg was a stupid asshole who didn't know a good thing when he had it. I can't help that," Pucci said.

I shook his hand away from my hair. "Look, I'm not some promiscuous little slut that sleeps with every man who asks. . . ."

"I've noticed," he said, his hand straying back to my hair.

"I know there was nothing gigantic going on between Cab and me. And I know Rea Carmody was just pulling my chain, but—"

"But I don't have to keep reminding you of it," Pucci finished for me, his hand moving to my neck, massaging the muscles there.

"Yeah, I guess," I said, forgetting what my point had been, the cars whizzing past us on the boulevard a blur.

"Do you want me to say something serious here?" Pucci asked.

"I don't think so," I answered, moving my head so his fingers could better dig into my flesh.

"Probably wouldn't be a good idea," Pucci said, his voice soft, his hand moving under the collar of my shirt, massaging the shoulder muscles. "Probably start something I'm not sure you could finish."

"Is that a dare?" I said, finally looking at him.

You know how it is when you are absolutely certain someone is going to kiss you? How you can see it coming, as he's moving his head closer to yours? How you can feel the little sparks of electricity flying between you? How you start to move toward him, start to close your eyes, wondering how his lips are going to feel, how he'll taste? If that heavy growth of beard will be scratchy or soft? If you'll have to forgo makeup after a few passionate kisses and the resultant whisker burn?

That's about where we were in the little tango Pucci and I had been engaged in when the police cruiser pulled up behind us with a little blast of its siren and flash of light.

We both sat back abruptly as the uniform got out of the cruiser and sauntered up to Pucci's window, his hand on his gun butt, his cap pulled low over his eyes.

"See your license, sir?" the cop said as Pucci rolled down his window.

Pucci pulled out his little leather folder with the badge and ID and showed it to the uniform.

"Oh." The cop straightened up. "Hey, Detective Pucci. Sorry. Saw this car parked on the verge . . . thought there might be some trouble."

"Little car trouble, that's all. I think I've got it running now, though."

The cop gave him a half-assed salute. "Great. Sorry to have bothered you," he said, and walked back to the car.

Pucci started the engine, checked the rearview mirrors, and pulled out into traffic.

13

We ended up at the police station. I sat in the visitor's chair next to Pucci's desk while he pecked away with two fingers on a computer keyboard. After fifteen excruciatingly boring minutes of studying the lay of Pucci's desk (i.e., his grotesquely stained coffee cup with the legend COPS DO IT WITH AUTHORITY; three books—*The City of Chicago Municipal Codes and Their Meaning to You, Firearm Maintenance,* and *Indigenous Male Police Personnel and the Women Who Love Them;* and a battery of wanted posters of some of the scummiest-looking people I've ever seen—plus one incredibly cute guy wanted for mail fraud), I got up and wandered down the hall in search of a candy machine. I found one, deposited sixty cents, and was rewarded with an almost petrified Baby Ruth. Since it has always been my theory that bad food has no calories, I deposited another sixty cents and got a graying Hershey's bar to go with it.

I got back to Pucci's desk just as he said, "Ah-ha."

"Ah-ha?"

"Ah-ha." He hit a key and a printer started up in the corner of the squad room. He stood up, went to the printer, waited while it finished, then ripped off the sheet and brought it over to his desk.

He handed it to me. It was a rap sheet on Rea Carmody. Two arrests for possession of cocaine, one arrest for intent to buy cocaine from an undercover cop, no convictions.

I handed back the paper and said, "Ah-ha." One thing about Pucci and me, I thought, we do give good repartee. "Your theory, o great detective," I said.

"Bucky Schwartz scored dope for more than just Cab. He was Carmody's supplier, too. You'll notice these arrests are all from about four years ago. It's obvious she's got a steady supplier now. . . ."

"Or she gave it up," I theorized.

"Ha. Once a doper, always a doper."

"And you send people to the penitentiary."

He raised an eyebrow.

"*Penitentiary,*" I said in my vastly superior way, "is from the old Protestant ethic of penitence."

"Catholics invented penitence."

"And the first penitentiaries were erected so that wrongdoers could go someplace and become penitent and be forgiven for their sins."

"And you brought up all this for what reason?" Pucci asked.

"To make you feel humiliated for assuming 'once a doper, always a doper.' People do repent."

"Bull. They just change one addiction for another. You know how many born-again Christians are ex-somethings? Dopers, drinkers, gamblers, wife-beaters, you name it."

"Well, maybe the Carmody changed her doping habit for bulimia."

He shrugged. "I like my scenario better."

"You would."

"Bucky's her supplier. Something happens in Atlanta—"

"What?"

"I don't know. Something. Anyway, she goes bonkers—"

"This isn't washing. Why would she kill her supplier?"

Pucci threw the rap sheet up in the air, along with his hands. "What's with you, Kruse?"

I folded my hands across my chest. "Oh, I don't know, Pucci. I just thought maybe finding out the *truth* might be more fun than making up crap as we go along."

He picked up the rap sheet from the floor and brandished it in my face. "Is this not a rap sheet?"

"It's a rap sheet."

"Does it not say that Rea Carmody was busted three times in drug-related incidents?"

"It says that."

"So . . ."

"So what has that got to do with the price of peanuts in Plains?"

"Nice alliteration."

"Thank you."

We glared at each other. I wondered if he wanted to bite my earlobe as much as I wanted to bite his.

"Then why," I asked, "did she come to the Lake House looking for Bucky Schwartz?"

"Because he's her connection."

"Then she obviously didn't kill him."

"Maybe she didn't kill him. Maybe they're in this together—"

"Then why is she looking for him?" I asked.

"Because . . . because . . ." Pucci slapped his hand on his desk top and leaned back in his chair. "Because I haven't got the foggiest notion."

"Okay. Maybe he's her connection but he double-crossed her."

"You really like this? Switching sides all the damn time? You're driving me nuts."

"Not a long trip. I was in debate in high school."

"Have a lot of teenage suicides that year?" Pucci asked, one eyebrow doing its thing.

"Okay. I have an idea."

"I can hardly wait."

"Listen." I took a deep breath. "I go back over to the Carmody's. By myself. I say, 'Listen, Rea, baby, we gotta talk. . . .' "

"And she spills her guts."

"Natch." I sat back and grinned.

"No," he said with all the authority vested in a minor public official.

"Pucci."

"No."

I stood up. "Well," I did an exaggerated stretch, thankful to see Pucci didn't take his eyes off the jeans and top, "I guess I'd better head back to the Lake House. It's getting late." I yawned.

"You're Saran Wrap, Kruse," Pucci said.

God, I wish I could raise one eyebrow. Instead, I raised both.

"Easy to see through," he interpreted.

"How droll. How clever. What a command you have of the English language. May I sit at your knee and learn from you?" I said.

"You can sit at or on any extremity I've got."

I stood up. "Well . . ."

"Well nothing. Sit down," Pucci commanded. I sat. "You're not going to Carmody's," he said.

"Of course not."

"It's a stupid idea," he said.

"Of course it is."

"You're not going to do it!" he said.

"Of course not."

"Kruse."

I stood up. "I need to get back." Pucci started to stand up, but I shooed him down. "Don't bother. I'll take a cab. You've got work to do."

He finished standing up, put his hand on my shoulder, and pushed me into the chair I'd just vacated.

"Kimmey, listen, this isn't a game. People are really dead." He cleared his throat and looked at the blank computer terminal. "I don't want you dead."

Jeeze. He called me Kimmey and didn't want me dead, both in practically the same sentence. It must be love.

"Pucci, I think this will work."

"It's a dumb idea."

"So what brilliant idea do you have?" I asked.

"I'll go with you."

"And we'll get as much information as we did last time. Which was all gotten by me, if the truth be known."

"What? That she's possibly bulimic?"

We glared at each other. I wondered if he worked out and had nice pecs under all the hair I assumed he had on his chest.

"I'm coming in with you," Pucci said.

"No! You can't. It's gotta be girl talk," I said, opening the door of his civvie car.

He opened his door. "I'll wait in the hall," he said.

"Of the penthouse? She'll see you. You go in the building and the guard will tell her you're here. You have to stay in the car, Pucci. You really, really do."

"And what if you need help?"

"I'll yell."

"All the way down from the twenty-second floor as you're being thrown off the balcony? At least I'll have a nice view," he said. "Too bad you're not wearing a dress."

"Sit," I commanded. "Stay." He sat back down in the car seat. "Good boy," I said, heading for the door of the Carmody's building.

It was the same guard and I told him I needed to see Rea Carmody again. He smiled and called her and, when she obviously agreed for me to come up, pointed in the direction of the elevator.

A uniformed patrolman sat in a folding chair in the foyer, a paperback in his hand, his head bent forward, ignoring the Carmody, who had the apartment door open and was leaning against the doorjamb, obviously waiting for me. She'd changed her power suit for a silk kimono and ballet slippers. Her makeup and hair, however, were still impeccable.

"What is it now?" she asked.

I exited the elevator and stood in front of her, as she obviously wasn't moving to let me in the apartment. "Just wanted to come by and apologize for earlier."

"Which part of earlier?" she asked. "You and your boyfriend barging in and asking dumb questions, or you searching my bedroom?"

I opened my mouth to protest, then thought better of it.

She moved away from the door and inside the apartment. I followed, closing the door quietly behind me.

She threw herself down on the tuxedo sofa and grabbed a cigarette, lighting it and tossing the gold Dunhill back on the table. "I could have you arrested for what you did in my bedroom."

I nodded my head. "I know. That was shameless of me. But I've never been in an apartment like this and—"

She snorted a laugh. "Stop the humble crap, Kruse." She sat up abruptly. "I can't believe you went through my things! I feel like throwing everything away and buying new!"

I shrugged. "Well, if you can afford it."

"I'm serious!" she said, her voice almost rising to a scream.

I leaned back in the black leather slingback chair. Unfortunately, my feet left the floor, which always makes me feel at a disadvantage, so I sat back up again. "I guess I was looking for something that would tell me why you lied."

Rea sat back on the couch. "Lied about what?"

I found it interesting that she didn't deny having lied at all. It sounded to me like she wondered which lie she'd been caught at.

"When you came to see me at the Lake House. That bull about Cab dumping you."

She shrugged. "He didn't actually dump me, no. He was supposed to spend the night that night. But when he ran into you at the club, he decided to sleep elsewhere." Again, she shrugged. "It *had* happened before. Too many times to count." She smiled. "Of course, this time it killed him."

Uh oh, I thought. Did she just confess? "So you killed him?"

Rea put her head back and laughed. "I'd hardly kill someone over sex. It's too readily available."

I noticed for the first time that the long, elegant brown cigarette shook in her hand. I also noticed that the lead crystal ashtray on the coffee table was heaped with half-smoked cigarette butts. Rea was nervous about something. Very nervous.

"Then why did you kill him?" I asked.

She sat up and looked at me. "I didn't."

"Something's going on, Rea. You're very nervous about something. What is it?"

She stood up and walked toward the front door of the apartment. "Get out, Kimmey. And please don't come back. All we have in common is having shared the same penis. It's hardly a bond." She opened the door and stood there, elegant, aloof, her hand shaking so badly the cigarette ash fell to the marble floor of the foyer. I left.

"He almost kissed me," I said.

"Almost only counts in horseshoes and hand grenades," Phoebe said.

"Hmm," I said.

"So?" she said.

"So what?" I said.

"So did he almost kiss you because you threw your head back and slapped his face or did he almost kiss you because he thought about it and decided it wasn't a good idea or what?"

"He almost kissed me because we were in his car on the side of the road and a cop stopped us."

"It's against the law to kiss in Illinois?"

"No, it's against the law to park on the verge, I guess," I said.

"So?"

"So what?"

"Would you have thrown your head back and slapped his face if the cop hadn't shown up?"

"It's a moot point now, Phoebe."

"Any more murders?"

"Nary a one," I said.

"Things are getting dull up there. What's happening?"

So I filled her in on my two trips to Rea Carmody's penthouse and the resultant information.

"Oh, and Pucci's decided it would be a good idea if I look after Babe when she leaves the hospital, which will be tomorrow. I talked to Max and Tracy and they said no problem. They're moving us to adjoining rooms."

"Is he going to have a guard there?"

I shrugged. "I don't know. I'll have to ask."

"Kimberly! You're not going to guard a woman who's already been victimized by this crazy once all by yourself. Do you hear me?"

"Yes, Mother."

"I'm serious."

"I know. I'll ask Pucci first thing in the morning. Look, I'm getting sleepy. It's been a long day. Talk to you tomorrow."

"If you live that long," my friend Phoebe said.

14

The bus stopped about two blocks from the Carlton. Ordinarily, it would have stopped in front of the door, but it was raining. And not just a gentle spring drizzle either, but a Midwest torrential downpour. I jumped off the bus and headed for the cover of a shop a few feet away. Awnings protected most of the distance between me and the Carlton, with gaps between stores and at alleyways. I huddled in my Salvation Army peacoat, my pink and orange retro leggings getting soaked from the rain blowing in under the awnings. Lightning lit the dull gray sky and thunder rumbled like my father's stomach after an enchilada dinner. If I hadn't been on a mission of mercy, I would have hailed a cab and gone back to the Lake House, but, there you go. I'm basically a decent person.

It was my job to pack up Babe Marsh's belongings. Pucci would be by to fetch them and me at noon and drive us to the hospital to get Babe to go back to the Lake House, where we would be met (putting Phoebe's mind at ease) by a very large, very mean, very armed policeman.

I was one awning and an alleyway away from the Carlton's front door when I spotted Joey Scarlotti and Bobby Rivers standing by said door engaged in a heated discussion. So heated Bobby shoved Joey and Joey reared back to hit Bobby.

I yelled, "Hey, fellas, having fun?"

They looked toward me. "Watch it, Bobby," Joey said loudly, "it's the slut that slays."

"Great alliteration," I yelled back, determined not to let this second rate Dice-man get to me. I stepped into the alleyway, looking down it to make sure no cars were coming. Under an awning by a side door, I saw a man, medium height, a little heavyset, dark curly hair.

"Bucky!" I yelled. I looked quickly to Bobby and Joey and pointed down the alley. "It's Bucky!"

Bobby and Joey ran around the side of the alleyway and went charging down it, with me hot on their heels. Bucky saw us and lit out in the other direction.

By the time the three of us got to the end of the alley, we were totally soaked. And Bucky was nowhere in sight.

"Are you sure it was him?" Pucci asked.

"Of course I'm sure," I replied.

"Yeah, it was him all right," Bobby said.

"No mistaking the little kike," Joey added.

"Did you see which way he went?" Pucci asked.

We all shook our heads. It had been raining so hard, and we'd been running with such abandon, we'd missed which way he'd gone.

Pucci went over and talked to a couple of uniforms in plastic-covered apparel and they nodded and headed toward the end of the alley.

He came back and took my arm. To Bobby and Joey, he said, "You two go on back to your rooms." As they left, he turned to me, "Do you want to go get Babe's things now, or would you rather go back to your hotel and change?"

"Hotel," I answered, shivering in my wet clothes. He took off his trench coat and draped it over my shoulders. "I'm freezing to death," I said. "I need to change into something dry."

"On one condition," he said.

I looked at him. "What?"

He grinned, "That I get to watch."

The streets were Texas-sized mud lakes as we headed back to the Lake House. The wind shook the car and the lightning and thunder rumbled around us.

"So," I said, "so much for our 'Rea Carmody is the killer and she also killed Bucky' theory."

Pucci shrugged. "I never put much stock in that theory," he said.

I didn't remind him it had been his own. A man needs some pride.

"So what do you think now, o great detective?"

He looked over at me. "That's good. Even shivering and shaking you can still act like a smart ass. It makes me proud, Kruse."

"Theories, Pucci. Theories."

He shrugged again. "A lot of people are dead. A lot of other people could have done it." He looked at me. "How's that?"

He swerved around a rain-filled pothole and said, "By the way, there was a phone report on my desk a while ago. They found Lorette Binz."

I twisted in my seat to look at him. "Is she okay?"

He smiled. "She's fine. Had car trouble, ended up sleeping on the road one night. But she's safe and sound in her hotel room in Pittsburgh now. Under police guard."

I leaned back in my seat. "Thank God," I said. I thought about the phone call I'd overheard between Bert Kaiser and his anonymous backer. "Pucci," I said, "there's something I've been meaning to tell you. . . ."

He hit the steering wheel with the heel of his hand. "Shit! You did it! I knew it! Now I'll have to arrest you and my chances of getting you in the sack are gonna get real slim."

"Stop acting like an undersexed eighth-grader. This is serious," I said.

He looked at me, his face somber. "Everything I say to you is said with the utmost sincerity and seriousness. Not to mention forthrightness, goodness, and niceness."

"Drop dead, Pucci."

"If you'd said that to me a couple of days ago, I might have," he said.

"Look," I said, trying to get back on track as he twisted the steering wheel tightly to the right, avoiding a large body of moving water and managing to knock me into him, even with my seat belt fastened, "right after Cab was killed, like two days after, I went to the comedy club to talk with Bert and, well, he was on the phone and he didn't see me so I sorta—"

"Eavesdropped?"

"Well, I didn't want to be rude and go barging in there while he was on the phone!"

"I've noticed that about you, Kruse. You are always incredibly polite."

"Thank you."

"That was sarcasm. . . ."

"I recognized it. I'm a professional, you know. Anyway," I said, trying to get him to shut up, which was an extremely difficult thing to do, "he was talking with someone and he said something like, 'It's been taken care of.' "

"What's been taken care of?" Pucci asked.

I shot him a look. "If I knew *that* we wouldn't be having this conversation. Shut up. Anyway, he said he'd 'done it,' whatever 'it' is, and then the guy on the other end of the phone threatened him. . . ."

"How do you know that?"

I sighed. "Because Bert said, and I quote, 'Don't threaten me!' Okay?"

"Oh. Okay."

"Then Bert threatened him. . . ."

"How? What did he say?" Pucci asked, his attention finally garnered.

I shrugged. "God, I don't remember exactly. Something like, 'If I go down, you go down,' or words to that effect."

Pucci nodded. We drove silently for a minute.

Not being able to stand it, I said, "Well? What do you think?"

"I think you should have told me this a while back."

"It sorta . . . slipped my mind."

"Um-hum."

"Well?"

Pucci pulled up to the front door of the Lake House, double-parking in the street. He pulled the cherry-top flasher out from under the dash and put it on the roof of the car and started the light flashing. Then we got out.

"I'll have a talk with Bert Kaiser," Pucci said, escorting me into the Lake House.

"Can I go with you?" I asked.

"No," he said, pushing me onto the elevator. "Let's get you changed into some dry clothes. And remember: I get to watch."

I had two potted ivies, a potted geranium, and a leaky vase of cut flowers in my arms as we headed for the hospital elevator. Pucci was carrying a sack with the least bloodstained clothes Babe had been wearing during her attack, a sack of prescription drugs and her hospital setup (a plastic tray, a plastic pitcher, and a box of tissue, all for the addition of only seventy-five dollars to Babe's hospital bill), and a philodendron. Babe, decked out in the outfit I'd brought her from her hotel room, rode in the wheelchair with the vase of flowers I'd given her and a dried arrangement her mother had sent from Ohio.

We made it downstairs to the pay-up window, where Babe haggled gently with the women behind the counter, who had never heard of Babe's insurance company. In less than an hour, we were out of there, heading for Pucci's unmarked squad car parked illegally in the emergency-room area.

"Oh, it's so good being out of there!" Babe said.

I smiled. "I'll bet. Lord, I hate hospitals."

Babe laughed. "Try being my size and sleeping on one of those awful beds!"

We got Babe in the front seat of the car and me in the back with Babe's luggage from her hotel, and headed toward the Lake House.

"Babe, I have to warn you, it's not what you're used to," I said. "It's, well, it's—"

"A dump," Pucci said.

"A little seedy," I said, pinching him on the back of the neck.

"It'll be fun!" Babe declared. "Just us girls roughing it!"

"Right," I said, staring glassy-eyed at our over-sized Pollyanna. I asked Pucci, "Did you ever find out what Joey and Bobby were fighting about?" On the way back to my hotel, I'd told him what I'd witnessed just before spotting Bucky Schwartz.

"When have I had time?" Pucci said. "I passed the word on to my fellow detectives and they'll find out. Believe me."

I sat back and ruminated. Fisticuffs under the awning of the Carlton. Over a taxi? Money? A girl? A gig? What else was there in the one-dimensional world of stand-up comedy? Dope? Had they known Bucky was back there all along? They were in front of me, blocking my view of Bucky as we ran down the alley. Could they have intentionally shielded him, their supplier? Or had I been watching too much television? I closed my eyes and grabbed a catnap.

We got to the hotel, and I wasn't so sure if Phoebe was going to like our protection. Our very large, very mean, very armed policeman had turned out to be a five-foot-five-inch blue-eyed blond nymphette with an attitude, who batted her lashes big-time at Pucci. She did, however, have a very powerful-looking gun on her Barbie-doll hip. Babe and I left her sitting in a straight-back chair against the wall between our two doors and settled into our rooms. I'd been moved again, this time to a room with an adjoining one so that Babe and I could be closer together and easier to protect.

I put away my things and lay down on the bed, contemplating the world and when I would get to be part of it again.

"Yoo-hoo!" Babe called, sticking her head out between the connecting doors of our rooms.

I could tell this was going to be loads of fun. How long did Pucci suppose we could all stay in Chicago? Indefinitely? If they didn't catch some-body soon, I'd either be walking back to Austin or into a loony bin due to the proximity of Babe Marsh.

Austin, I thought, oh, Lord, to be back in Aus-tin. Sunsets at the Oasis, spitting on the houses downhill from Mount Bonnell, a night of music at Antone's or a walk down Sixth Street, canoeing on Town Lake, water-skiing on Lake Austin, sailing on Lake Travis, hot-air balloon races, and Eyeore's Birthday Party. Good God, did I miss home.

"Hey, Babe," I said, sitting up slightly from my prone position on the bed.

"Anybody home?" she said, coming in and flopping down on the love seat.

"Just us chickens," I said, lying down on my side facing her, so as not to be rude. "You all settled in?"

"Oh, I hardly have anything. It was no big deal."

Since I'd packed all her belongings at the Carlton, I knew exactly what she had, which was enough, when packed in the three suitcases I'd found in her closet, to give Pucci a running start at a hernia.

I had no idea what I was going to do with her. X number of days stuck in a hotel room with Babe Marsh could turn me into a jelly doughnut. But, as sweet, sweet, sweet as she was, I still kind of liked her.

"So," I asked Babe, "what got you into this biz?"

"Doing stand-up?" She shrugged her massive shoulders. "Oh, I don't know. Everybody always said I was funny." She laughed self-consciously. "Does the expression 'fat and jolly' ring any bells?"

"You know," I said, trying to be delicate, "you've got some really good material. . . ."

"Oh, not as good as yours. Are you hungry?"

"I'm always hungry. You want me to call room service?"

"Maybe just some snacks?"

I got off the bed and went to the door and opened it. Barbie—I mean Rochelle—sat in a straight-back chair between the doors of my room and Babe's, reading a Joseph Wambaugh novel. "You want some food? We're ordering room service."

She stood and stretched, her uniform doing things to her body that I was glad Pucci was not there to witness, and said, "Maybe a salad?"

What a wimp, I thought, as the two of us moved back into my room to the phone to order.

Us three girls sat around and made small talk while waiting for our orders. Finally, after about twenty minutes, there was a knock on the door. As I stood to answer it, Rochelle put out one arm to stop me as the other went to the gun on her hip.

"I'll get it," she said, moving menacingly to the door. It was Tracy, laden with food—fried cheese sticks and stuffed mushrooms for Babe, a cheeseburger, fries, onion rings, and a malt for me, and a salad with oil and vinegar for Rochelle.

Rochelle excused herself and took her salad back to her chair, leaving Babe and me alone. Probably couldn't stand the close proximity of all those calories.

As Babe and I devoured our repasts, I started up again. "Talking about your routine . . ."

"Well, I try. I'm glad you like it."

"I do. I was just wondering, though," I said, "why you tell all those, well, fat jokes?"

Babe looked up at me, her brown eyes large in her face, pretty eyes portraying a pretty soul, all wrapped up in something warm and wiggly. "Beat 'em to the punch," she said, her voice small.

"What?"

She swallowed a mushroom whole and looked at me. "When I was in junior high, the other kids started making fun of me because of my size. I found the best way to stop them was to start it myself."

She looked at me and I nodded my encouragement.

Babe sighed. "I'd make a joke about being fat, you know, say something like, 'Gosh, that's a cute dress, can I borrow it for a belt?' You know, like that."

I laughed.

"That way," she said, "they laughed with me. Not at me."

I got up from the bed and moved to her, putting my arms around her and hugging her. It was an impulse. And one I'm not sorry I gave into.

She hugged me back and then held me at arm's length. Smiling, she said, "What was that for?"

"Because I think you're a hell of a lady and very funny to boot."

Babe blushed and grinned. "Yeah?" she said.

"Yeah," I said.

15

I called room service for some hot chocolate and Tracy's scrumptious chocolate truffle cheesecake and told Babe, "We need to do something here."

"What's that?"

"Well, if we don't figure out who in the hell is doing all this, Pucci's liable to keep us in Chicago till I get a Yankee accent, and, God knows, we don't want that to happen."

Babe laughed. "Yuck, that would be unpleasant!"

"Besides, I've got a gig in Baton Rouge next week and I'd like to get home in between to feed the cat and water the plants, know what I mean?"

"Who's doing that now?" Babe asked.

"My landlady."

"Well, I know what you mean, though. . . . My

mother's not all that well and I hate leaving her alone all this time," Babe said.

"So," I said, "we need to do something."

"What is it you propose we do?"

I shrugged. "Figure it out. With both our brains, we should be able to find out who did this a hell of a lot quicker than Pucci and the rest of the Chicago PD."

Babe laughed. "Us? What is this? *Kimmey Kruse, Girl Detective, and Her Faithful Indian Companion?*"

I thought about it. Then grinned. "Not bad. I like it. Top billing and all."

She tossed a pillow at me. "You're cute, but you're weird."

I sat up on the bed. "No. I'm serious. What do you know about the principals in this thing? Joey and Bobby? Bucky? That bitch Carmody? And don't try to be nice. I want the real dope here."

Babe leaned back in the love seat. "Hmmm, well, speaking of dope . . ."

"What?"

"Well . . ."

"Babe! Spill it."

"Well, you know I said I worked with Joey in Omaha. When he and his girlfriend had that fight?"

"Right?"

"Well, I went to his room one night to give him a message from someone and when he opened the door, I could see the girl sitting at the table with a line of coke and a straw . . . so . . ."

I leaned back on my pillows. "Okay," I said, "we got Cab doing coke, according to Carmody. Also, according to Carmody, we got Bucky

Schwartz supplying Cab with the coke. And, by past record, we have Carmody doing coke. Now we have Joey doing coke. What about Bobby?"

Babe shrugged. "I don't know. I never saw him doing any. I only worked with him once at that Canadian gig and there were so many people there, you didn't get to know anybody, really. The only thing I know about Bobby that you might not know is that he speaks Spanish."

"No kidding? Well, so do I, sorta, because I'm from Texas. I took it in high school and in college. And Bobby's from southern California, right?"

Babe nodded. "I think so." There was a knock on the door. "Oo, goody, there's the food."

I went to the door, where Rochelle Supercop stood with a tray. Tracy was headed for the elevator. "Thanks, Trace!" I called, and she smiled and waved back.

"Is she still eating?" Rochelle whispered to me, obviously an obesophobic.

I glared at her. "It's for me," I said, and slammed the door in her face. Some people can be so prejudiced. But I got to admit, Babe was one of the few people who could keep up with me in calories.

I took the tray to the bed, where we both grabbed our goodies. "Okay," I said. "If he's from southern California, it's not surprising he speaks Spanish. A lot of Californians do, just like Texans. Being so close to Mexico and all. But what has that got to do with anything?"

"Nufin'," Babe said around a mouthful of chocolate truffle cheesecake. She swallowed. "That's just all I know about him. When I asked him how come he spoke Spanish so fluently, he said it was because of the maid they had when he was a kid. Now, this is weird."

"What?" I said, between mouthfuls.

"He said they had this maid from the time he was about two years old until he left for college—and he said, 'Rosella, Roserita, something like that.' Can you believe it? I mean, isn't that . . . well, shallow?" She blushed and held her hand in front of her mouth. "Oh, Lord, get me started and I turn into a real gossip!"

"That's more than shallow, Babe, that's disgusting. Sixteen years and he can't remember her first name? Just the hired help, right?"

"Well, maybe it was because she was only there when he was in school and he never saw her."

"He learned Spanish though, right?"

"Oh," Babe said. "That's right." She looked at me and her face got serious. "He's an asshole."

I giggled. "Way to go, Babe!" Sobering, I said, "Okay. Bobby Rivers. He's an asshole and he's probably prejudiced."

"Definitely." Babe said, slurping her hot chocolate.

"And he was forced to give up a gig to Cab. . . ."

"Yeah! What about that? That gives him a hell of a motive!"

I grinned. "Now you're getting with the program, Babe. Everybody's guilty but us!"

She held up her arm in the old Black Power salute and said, "Righteous!"

"But—okay, that gives him a motive for killing Cab. But what about the others?"

Babe finished her hot chocolate and put the mug down on the tray. "Hmmm, let's see. Maybe he was up for the gig in Atlanta and he didn't get it and he was mad at everybody who was there?"

"Weak," I said, finishing my own hot chocolate and putting the mug on the tray next to hers. "What do all of you have in common other than the gig in Atlanta?"

Babe shrugged. "We're comedians. Some male, some female. We're all white. No, Don Resson was black. Okay, different sexes, different races, different religions. All the same occupation. All in the same place at the same time."

"When? Maybe it's the date, not the place!"

"The last week in February," Babe said.

"After Valentine's? After Presidents' Day? Was this year a leap year?" I grabbed my purse and looked at my calendar. "No. Was something going on somewhere else?"

"I don't know. This is giving me a headache." She lay down on the love seat, her feet hanging over the edge.

"Here," I said, scooting over, "come lie up here so you can be comfortable."

As she was getting herself resituated, the phone rang. I picked it up.

"Hello?" I said.

"Kimmey?"

It was a man's voice. Faintly familiar, but not recognizable.

"Yes?"

"Are you alone?"

"Who is this?" I asked.

"Shh, be quiet!"

"Bucky?" I whispered, my heart running around in my chest like a gerbil in a cage.

Babe sat up next to me, her eyes wide.

"Shh, listen! I've got to talk to you!" he said.

"Where are you?"

"Don't tell anybody I called! Promise?"

"Yes, yes," I said, "I promise. Where are you?"

"Will you come here? Alone?"

"Why?" I asked, feeling my skin nub up in goose flesh.

"Because I didn't do anything! I've got to have somebody believe me! Kimmey, please, I'm scared shitless! Help me!"

"Okay, okay, calm down," I said. "But why did you run away today?"

"Because you were chasing me! You and those two baboons! Kimmey, I know you didn't kill Cab—now! And I know I didn't kill him! You've got to help me!"

I sighed. "What can I do?"

His voice rising with hysteria, Bucky whined, "Please, just come talk to me! I can't come there, somebody will see me and I'll get arrested and they'll put me in jail and then some big guys are going to do terrible things to me and even when they prove me innocent I'll be ruined for life because maybe I'll like it and then my entire heterosexual existence will have been a sham and—"

"After all you've done, why should I?" I asked.

There was a long silence. At least a minute's worth. Then he said, "Because I think I've figured it out."

"What?" My throat felt dry, my palms clammy. "Then call Pucci! He's the one—"

"No! He won't listen to me! He'll just hang my balls out to dry! But if you told him . . ."

"Forget it . . ." I started.

"No! Listen!" Bucky insisted. "I'll tell you what's going on, what I think happened . . . then you go to Pucci and pave the way for me turning myself in. It's the only way I'm going to do it."

"Okay. So tell me—"

"Not over the phone. It has to be in person. This is too hot, Kimmey, I swear."

I thought about it. "Okay," I said at last.

"You'll come? Alone? Not call that cop boyfriend of yours?" Bucky asked.

"He's not my boyfriend. And, yes, I'll come. Alone."

Bucky let out a sigh. "Great. Thanks. I mean it, Kimmey. And I'm really sorry I said things about you. I mean, you're great, you really are and I'll always—"

"Bucky! Where are you?"

"At the comedy club."

"Kaiser's?"

"Yes. I'll be in the main hall. Come, please!" And he hung up.

"You can't go alone!" Babe whispered.

I was getting dressed. Black leggings, a black Lycra bodysuit and my new glow-in-the-dark boxers for color. I grabbed my Green Bay garage-sale jacket. "I told him I would. Look, we could find out what happened and go to Pucci with it!"

Babe put her hands on her ample hips. "We've got to call Pucci!"

I looked at her. "You're joking."

"Do you see anybody with a paycheck? No, I'm not joking." She put her hand on the telephone. "We'll call Pucci and I'm going with you."

I looked at the door. "All right, already. But I need you to cover for me with the Barbie doll out there."

"We'll tell her we're going to bed . . . but how are we getting out of here?"

I grinned. "Don't worry your pretty little head. I know how to do that." I grabbed my bathrobe and slipped my feet into my Bullwinkle slippers. "The same way I dated a guy with a motorcycle all the way through high school with my parents never knowing. Except with an extra twist. Get a bathrobe on over your clothes," I told Babe.

She ran into her room and came back with robe and slippers and quickly put them on. I opened the door and smiled at Rochelle. "We're going to bed now, good night."

"Good night," Babe said, and waved for good measure.

" 'Night," Rochelle said, not taking her eyes off her book.

We shut the door and I said, "Like when you were a kid—pillows under the covers."

Babe looked blank for a moment then said, "Oh," and headed for her room.

I made a reasonable Kimmey-sized lump under the covers with the extra pillows and turned off the light, just as Babe came stumbling in from her darkened room.

"I tried to call Pucci," she said, "but he wasn't there, so I left a message."

"What'd you say?" I asked.

"I told the guy that answered that it was an emergency and for Pucci to meet the dynamic duo at the Kaiser KK asap."

"Dynamic duo?"

"Well, that's better than saying our names. What if the cop who answered knew about Rochelle?" Babe asked, wide-eyed, pointing toward the door on the other side of which sat our great protector, totally innocent of the plot going on behind her.

"Good thinking," I said.

"Now what?" she asked.

"Follow me," I said, heading for the bathroom. I turned on the light and opened the door to the small closet. Using a pair of scissors, I pried up the tile on the floor of the closet, revealing nothing.

"Well, damn," I said, sitting back on my haunches. "Oh, maybe it's your bathroom," I said, and rushed Babe out of my bathroom and out of my room into hers.

"What?"

"In high school with Scooter, the guy with the motorcycle, I had to shimmy down the pecan tree outside my bedroom window. But you'll notice Chicago is incredibly deficient in pecan trees. So . . . Tracy showed me one time right after they got the hotel. This used to be a house of ill repute back in the golden days and there are trapdoors in some of the rooms."

Once in Babe's bathroom closet, I pried up the tile—and there it was. A two-foot-by-two-foot-square trapdoor, nailed shut. I tried prying up the nails, but only succeeded in breaking the blade of the scissors.

❀ 195 ❀

"Here, let me," Babe said. She traded places with me and said, "Run water in the shower!"

I turned on the tap and ran back to see her smashing the old and rotting wood with the heel of her shoe. The wood gave way and landed with a thud in the darkness below.

"Just a second," Babe said, and ran back into her bedroom, returning seconds later with her purse. She brought out a penlight and flashed the beam of light through the opening. Below us was an identical bathroom closet, with the wood from the shattered trapdoor on the floor.

"Okay, wait," I said, running back into Babe's room. I grabbed the cushions from Babe's love seat and, after we were through picking the shards of broken wood away from the hole, stuffed the cushions through the hole. They landed in a heap on the floor of the closet of the room below.

"Okay," Babe said, "I'll go through first."

"Why you?"

"Because I might need help getting through this tiny hole."

"Oh. Okay."

Babe threw her purse over the edge then sat down on the side of the hole, her legs and feet dangling into the darkness, the penlight held in her teeth. "Ofkay, haw gawz nufkin."

Babe leaped off into space, only to get caught by her massive breasts. "Oh, thit," she said, levering her arms up to take the weight off her boobs and grabbing the penlight out of her mouth. "Okay, Kimmey, gimme your best!"

I put my hands on the top of her head and pushed with all my body weight. And Babe disappeared. A thud at the bottom let me know she'd landed. I stuck my head through the opening. "Are you okay?" I called.

"Yeah, but I broke the damned flashlight!" Babe whispered back.

16

There were no lights on at the Kaiser Komedy Klub and, like an idiot, I'd forgotten to ask Bucky which door would be unlocked. Loud rock music and drunken voices issued forth from the other clubs in the area, with an occasional screeching of tires as couples paired off and headed for their trysts.

What with all the street traffic and the front door of the club being as brightly lit as a gaggle of academics at a convention, we tried the side, the one the comics entered on work nights. It was unlocked, leading into a dark hallway. Babe grabbed my arm and we maneuvered our way down the black hall, touching the left wall for balance. We got to the wings of the stage—I could tell that by the feel of the backdrop curtains—but still no lights.

Tentatively, I called out, "Bucky?"

"You alone?" he answered back.

"Yes," I lied, feeling Babe's grip on my arm.

"You sure?" the voice from the darkness said.

"Bucky, it's just me," I said. "Now turn on some lights."

The stage was suddenly bathed in light. The empty, barren, lonely stage.

I took one gingerly step into the light. "Bucky?" There was no response from wherever he was hiding. "You've got two seconds, Buckmeister, or I'm outa here," I said. "This isn't a hell of a lot of fun."

He stepped out from the opposite wing. Bucky Schwartz, hair mussed, two days' growth of beard, shoes scuffed. "Okay," he said. "Here I am. You gonna have me arrested?"

"Right," I said, "let me read you your Miranda." I walked toward him. "I've got a few thousand questions to ask you, mister. Where have you been?"

Bucky blushed. "Well I met this girl at a bar and—"

"The most important question is why you attacked Babe!" I said, interrupting the reminiscences of his sex life.

Bucky turned toward me, looking at me. "I called Rea last night and she told me what's being said about me! That's why I called you! I didn't do anything to Babe!"

"That's right," Babe said, stepping out of the shadows. "He didn't."

Bucky and I both turned to look at her.

Bucky said, "Oh, shit," and started backing up.

That's when the gun in Babe's hand went off, hitting Bucky high in the chest, knocking him back into the wings, where he hit his head on a scaffolding and went down like a rock. The large electrical switch that controlled the lighting was right by where he went down. I leaped for it and turned off the lights. The Kaiser Komedy Klub fell into total darkness.

Another shot rang out and I felt the sting of the heat from the bullet as it whipped past my hip. I looked down instinctively—and saw my glow-in-the-dark boxer shorts glowing in the dark for all they were worth, the Easter eggs and bunnies as distinct in the total darkness as stars in the sky, but a lot closer.

I ran blindly away from where I knew Babe had been, jerking at the boxer shorts, trying to get them off. I tripped and fell just as the lights came back on.

"Please don't run, Kimmey," Babe said, standing there by the electrical switch, one hand on the switch, the other holding the gun on me.

I untangled the boxers from my feet and stood. "Well, Babe, now what?"

She shook her head and tears ran down her cheeks. "I don't want to kill you, Kimmey."

"Good," I said, "I don't want you to, either."

"You're my friend. The best friend I've ever had."

I could feel the tears stinging my eyes. "Then let me go," I said. "I won't tell. . . ."

She laughed. Not a good sign. "Yeah, right. Bucky's lying here bleeding to death and you're not going to tell anyone. I kill everybody and—"

"You didn't kill *everybody* . . ." I started.

She took her hand off the electrical switch to count on her fingers. "I killed Don Resson, and

Mike Burley, and Cab, and that jerk Mickey, and believe me, I'll finish off Bucky. . . ."

She turned toward him with the gun and I said, "Babe, wait! Okay, so you killed everybody. But why? Please just tell me why!"

She turned back to me, her eyes dry now. She laughed. "Oh, great, what is this, some Agatha Christie novel? The great denouement?"

"No, I've just got to know some things. Like who was it who hit you at your hotel?"

"Oh, that. I hired this guy I saw in a bar down the street from the Carlton. He worked there. The busboy. I gave him fifty dollars to come to my room. When I heard you knock, he hit me. It was all planned. How he'd get out and all. I just didn't plan for him to hit me so hard. The little creep seemed to enjoy it!"

"Where'd you get the digitalis you gave Cab and Don Resson?"

She rolled her eyes toward the ceiling. "My mother's old boyfriend, Mr. Hausferberger. He had a heart condition and he always kept an extra bottle of his medication at my mom's house. He kept it in my bathroom. My mom never goes in there. She didn't know it was there. I got a copy of the PDR at the library and figured out how much it would take. Unfortunately, there was only enough left in the bottle to kill two, maybe three people, but I wanted to make sure, so I used extra on both of them."

"Why plant the bottle on me?" I asked. "And why in the world would you still have it with you?"

Babe sighed. "We weren't exactly friends then,

Kimmey. And I had to get rid of it. Your purse was just lying there. I didn't know what else to do with it. I kept it in my pocket because I was afraid to throw it away or leave it in my room."

I pointed at the gun. "And where did that come from?"

"Gosh, you ask a lot of questions!" Babe shifted from one foot to the other, obviously tired of the game. "It was in my purse. You just never looked in there."

She was right. I hadn't.

She sighed and looked hard at me. "You're just stalling," she said. "You think that stupid Pucci is going to come to your rescue. . . ."

"I assume you lied about calling him?" I looked at her hard. "Friend."

Tears instantly sprang to her eyes and she leaned her head back, gulping in air in great sobs. "Oh, God! I just couldn't not do it, Kimmey. I couldn't let them. . . ."

Her shoulders racked with sobs. I moved toward her, but she straightened, holding the gun out at me, both hands steadying it.

"Don't," she said. "Just don't move."

I held my hands up in surrender. "I'm not, Marilyn, I'm not moving at all."

She laughed again. "Is that some cheap psychological trick? Calling me Marilyn? I'm supposed to break down and give you the gun?"

"No. You're just supposed to remember that I'm your friend. That I know who you really are."

"You don't know anything, Kimmey. You don't know what he did to me. . . ." She gulped in air again, her body shaking.

With a quick glance at Bucky, lying on the floor in an ever-widening pool of blood, I pointed at the steps from the stage to the audience. "Let's sit down. Keep the gun pointed on me if you have to, but let's at least get comfortable while we talk about this."

"I don't want to be comfortable. If I have to shoot you, the least I can be is uncomfortable," Babe said.

I moved slowly toward the steps, my back to her. "Come on," I said over my shoulder. "Let's sit down."

I moved until I found the first step, then sat gingerly on the stage, my feet resting on the first stair. Slowly, she came and joined me, the gun in the hand farthest from me, her body turned slightly so she could watch me.

"What did he do?" I asked.

She shook her head. "No. Everybody who knows that is dead now. Except for Bucky, and he's dying. So it's okay."

I touched her hand. "I used to have a best girlfriend back in Texas. Phoebe was her name. Phoebe and I told each other everything, because that's what best girlfriends do. The good things . . . and the bad things."

Again, she shook her head, but the tears had started again. "It was so awful. And I thought he was so nice."

"Bucky?" I said, trying to figure out what was going on.

She stiffened. "No, not Bucky! Your precious Cab!"

"He raped you?"

She shook her head. "Not legally. No. Not rape." She sighed. "I was a virgin. Did you know that?"

I shook my head. "No, I didn't know that."

"A thirty-five-year-old virgin." She looked down at her body. "But then, who'd want to make love to this, right?"

"That's not true—"

"Oh, shut up. Don't humor me just because I have a gun."

"Okay, then," I said, "put the gun down and let's talk turkey."

"Fat chance," she said. Then laughed. "Fat chance. Get it?"

Babe sighed and looked at me. "He had that mole on the back of his left thigh. Remember?"

I remembered. I nodded.

"I kissed it. Put my tongue on it. It tasted salty, like the rest of his body. Atlanta . . ." She looked off into space. "He was so wonderful to me. The first two days. He called me Rubenesque. You know what that means?"

I nodded. "Rubens painted big, beautiful women."

She nodded rapidly. "Yes. That's right. Cab said I was Rubenesque. Big and beautiful. He'd come off stage and touch my hair and smile at me. The second night, he came off stage and he kissed me, right in front of everyone. I thought at first I'd peed my pants. But it wasn't that. It was . . . well . . ."

"I know." I said.

She laughed. "Yes, I'm sure you do." She sighed. "He took me back to his bus. And we made love. For hours. And he was so gentle and sweet. I thought I'd died and gone to heaven.''

"Cab was never the type to stay with one woman, Babe.''

She turned to me quickly, so quickly I almost jumped. "Oh, I knew that! I knew it was a one-time thing! But just to have that night! Just to have someone love me that one night . . .''

"Then why? Why all . . . this?''

She looked away from me, her eyes tearing up again, great balls of tears falling down her cheeks. "The third night, the last night, they were in the men's dressing room . . . Cab, and Don Resson, and Mike Burley, and Mickey Reynolds, and Bucky . . . all in there together. I was alone in the women's dressing room. . . . They didn't know I was there. It wasn't much of a dressing room. One of those plastic partitions cutting off the two sections. You could hear everything going on in the other room. . . .''

She stood up and walked back to Bucky, holding the gun pointed down at him. I ran up to her.

"Babe! No, please! What happened?''

She turned on me, whipping the gun around. She grabbed my hair and pulled me to her, the gun poking me sharply in the abdomen. Finally, the hand in my hair relaxed, and she leaned her forehead against mine.

"I love you, Kimmey,'' she said.

I touched her hair, keeping to the side away from the gun. "I love you, too, Babe,'' I said, the tears stinging my eyes.

She let go of me and walked away, her back to me. I thought of running, but I couldn't. "Babe?'' I said.

With her back to me, facing a nonexistent audience, she said, "They were laughing. Laughing their heads off. The partition wasn't fastened all the way and I peeked through to see what was going on. They were watching TV. In between the laughing, I could hear the TV. Moaning. Lots of moaning. Then a woman . . . saying . . . things . . ."

She turned and looked at me. "I've recorded my voice enough in practice sessions to know what I sound like on tape, Kimmey."

"Oh, Jesus," I said, the tears running down my face.

She turned with her back to me again, and I knew it was too painful to share with me face to face. She sighed. "And the others . . . Don Resson, I think, said, 'Oh, Jesus, man, that's the grossest thing I've ever seen.' And Bucky . . ." She looked over to where he lay bleeding and unconscious on the floor. "Bucky shook his head, and made a retching noise and said, 'All that flab, man . . .'" She gulped in a sob. "And then Cab got up and pointed at something on the screen, and he said, 'See this? Is that unbelievable or what? It's the only thing little about that cow.' When he moved I could see the TV screen. See myself. Oh, God, it was . . . awful. And they were all laughing. Don, and Bucky, and Mickey and Mike. They all laughed. And then the picture went to snow for an instant, and then there was Cab, on screen all by himself. He was working out a routine. Hand motions . . . body language. All about me. And they all thought it was so funny." She sighed. "It took all the courage I had, but I went in there, knocking them over as I went, and I pulled the tape out of the machine and I smashed the cassette with my foot and tore at the tape until it was all shredded." She turned to me. "None of them would look at me. Kimmey, how could I not kill them?"

She dropped the gun to the floor and walked over to the stairs and sat.

I picked up the gun and went to Bert's office and called Pucci.

A misty fog had moved in, blanketing the parking lot of the Kaiser Komedy Klub in an eerie glow from the shrouded streetlamps. The sound of the rock music and drunken laughter was both piercingly loud and strangely muted. I stood under the awning of the side door, Pucci's arm protectively around my shoulders.

They had her hands behind her back, the handcuffs cutting into the flesh of her wrists. I pushed Pucci's hand away. "They're hurting her, dammit! Take the cuffs off!" I shouted, running toward the squad car where the uniformed officer was taking Babe.

The angry flashing lights of the ambulance and the squad car ricocheted off the fog, arguing in the pale darkness.

Pucci grabbed my arm again. "Kimmey, don't. Honey, they have to. It's procedure. . . ."

I pulled away. "Damn your procedure!"

"Kimmey!" Babe called as the officer touched her head to lower her into the backseat of the squad car. "It's okay. It doesn't hurt." She smiled and disappeared inside the car.

I turned away from Pucci so he wouldn't see the tears.

* * *

"Did you ever find out what Joey and Bobby were arguing about?" I asked Pucci.

We sat in the coffee shop of the Lake House. Actually he was off duty. Just getting a head start on the next day's work. Interrogating witnesses. Excuse me, witness. Me.

He shrugged. "We had them in for questioning most of the night. Them and Rea Carmody. With Joey there, we knew we'd get them arguing sooner or later. And it worked. They all got pissed and started blaming each other. The essence of it was that Bucky was making some nice change on the side selling dope to everybody on the circuit who wanted any. Which seems to be everybody but you."

"Cocaine makes me nauseous," I said.

"It's also addictive and illegal," he said in his self-righteous way.

"What's going to happen to them?" I asked.

He shrugged. "Nothing," he said. "Bucky we could have busted. . . ." He looked at me, shrugging again. "But the others, well, we didn't catch 'em in the act. So . . ."

"Right," I said, leaning back against the chair, stretching my legs out under the table. All I wanted to do was sleep. For six weeks. A month. Maybe two.

"But I had Rea detained for a bit on a detail. Gonna have the police shrink have a look at her. See about a rehab program. The lady's got a monkey on her back the size of a gorilla."

"I noticed she seemed to be having some nerve problems when I was at her place." I leaned my head against my arm on the back of the chair. "Did you ever find out why she came by the Lake House to start with?"

He shrugged. "She told you the truth the first time. She was looking for Bucky. She wanted dope."

I closed my eyes, trying to shut out all the sights and sounds. Including the ones running nonstop behind my closed eyelids. The sight of Bucky Schwartz bleeding to death. The sound of Babe Marsh's terrible memories.

"Oh," he said, "by the way. One of the street cops put a report on my desk from earlier this evening. I couldn't help reading it while we were dealing with the great comedy doper ring."

"Am I interested in this?" I asked wearily.

"Shots were fired at Bert Kaiser's residence tonight."

I looked up. I was interested in this. "Is Bert okay?" I asked.

"Nobody was hit. Just seems Bert's new wife took a shot at him. According to the report, she's quite a hot little number. About twenty-two or so.

"Seems she found out about Bert and one of his backers—a banker named . . . I don't know, something that ended in 'ski.' Anyway, she caught them in bed. Which is something the banker's been wanting to have happen for a while. . . ."

"You think that's the conversation I heard?"

Pucci shrugged. "Coulda been."

We were silent for a while. Finally, Pucci said, "Why?"

"Why what?"

"Babe."

I shook my head. "I don't know," I said.

"She didn't say anything? Didn't give you any reason why she'd killed five men?"

I looked him straight in the eye. "I haven't a clue," I said.

Bucky Schwartz had been pronounced DOA. Had bled to death on the floor of the Kaiser Komedy Klub. That should bring Bert a few patrons, I thought. I didn't know Bucky, and what I had known I hadn't liked. But I'd watched him bleed to death, and that would be with me for the rest of my life.

But with Bucky dead, no one would know. Ever. Let them think she was crazy. And maybe she was, a little. If they could prove her crazy, she'd just go into a mental institution for a few years. And then . . .

I sighed and stood up. "I need a bath. Good night, Pucci."

He stood up as I left.

I lay in the tub, water as hot as I could stand stinging me and turning my body red. And I thought about Cab Neusberg. I had no problem believing what Babe had said. Cab was nice to me. Yes. To me he was nice. But about me? I don't know. If I had gone to Cab's bus instead of insisting he come to my hotel, would there have been a video of me? I didn't know. I'd never know.

But I was cute. A female, but cute. To the Cabs of this world, someone who looked like Babe wasn't even human. He only saw her vulnerability. He only saw his own use for her. An experiment. I could almost hear his thoughts. "Hum, never slept with a fat chick." New experiences. And new experiences mean new material.

Babe had spent her entire life making sure people laughed with her, not at her. And with one routine, Cab would have changed all that. The audience, the civilians, wouldn't know *whom* they were laughing at, but Babe would have known.

Did I blame Babe for what she had done? I didn't know. But I know I blamed Cab. Mickey and Bucky and Don and Mike. They had no right. But sometimes the mob mentality takes hold and what someone wouldn't do on their own, they'd do with a crowd. How did they feel when Babe came in the room and took the tape and destroyed it? Guilt? Shame? Embarrassment? For her or for themselves? They were all dead now. I'd never know.

Tomorrow, first thing in the morning, I was going home. Back to Austin and Phoebe and my folks. But I would come back to Chicago. I would sit on the stand at the trial, if there was one, and I would say I saw her shoot Bucky, because I had seen that. And I would say she then just handed me the gun. That's all. "Sorry, Judge, I don't know why." And God would forgive me that whopper.

I got out of the tub and dried off, scrubbing my body with the skimpy Lake House towel, and put on my jammies with the feet in them and the little trapdoor on the butt. I needed them tonight. And maybe a teddy bear to curl up with . . .

There was a knock on the door.

I peeked through the keyhole. Pucci.

I opened the door. "What?"

He stood there, two pillows under his arms. "This is your last night in Chicago," he said.

"Yeah? So?"

"So, we're gonna sleep together."

"Shit!" I started to slam the door, but he moved one pillow to the other arm and grabbed the door. He took my arm.

"Come on," he said, pulling me down the hall.

"I'm in my jammies!"

"And you look damned cute, too," he said.

He herded me into the elevator and down into the lobby and to one of the lobby couches, on which a worn blanket had been haphazardly thrown. He sat down and pulled me down with him. He spread the blanket over our laps, situated one pillow behind his head and one on his shoulder.

"Now," he said, "sleep with me."

A vacuum cleaner hummed from the other side of the lobby where Max was busy cleaning, and even busier trying not to notice us. The coffee shop was closed and dark, and only a night light showed behind the check in counter of the lobby. The overhead lights were muted. A hotel at rest in the middle of the night.

I could feel the texture of Pucci's suit coat through the thin flannel of my jammies. Could smell him, the smell of wool and male. A good smell. His arm rested gently on my shoulder, the fingers caressing.

"What did Phoebe say to you on the phone?" I asked, looking up into those cow brown eyes.

"She said, 'Be nice. She likes you.' "

"She's right," I said.

He kissed me. The kiss that had been interrupted for so long. And I was right. His heavy beard

stung my cheeks and his mouth tasted like pepper-
mint.

I snuggled up close to him, his arm protectively
around me, and said, "Did you hear about the Nazi
general who would line up the POWs every morning and make them shift from one foot to the other
saying only, 'tic-toc, tic-toc'?"

"No," he said in my ear. "Never heard it."

"Anyway, one day he's inspecting the line and
comes across this one POW saying 'tic-tic, tic-tic.'
Well, the Nazi gets really angry and shouts, 'Ve
have vays of making you toc!' "

"Puns are the lowest form of humor," he said.

"Really?"

"I have it on the highest authority," he said.

"Don't let me forget to pick up my new jacket
from the cleaner's in the morning," I said, yawn-
ing.

"Shut up, Kruse, and sleep with me," he said.

So I shut up and slept with Pucci.